Josie's Refuge

(Clearwater Daddies Book 3)
Alyssa Bailey
USA Today Bestselling Author
alyssabaileyromance.com

Also by Alyssa Bailey

Clearwater Daddies
Josie's Refuge (Second chance, Daddy)

Watch for more at alyssabailey.com.

Note from the Author

The third book in this series took a while to appear. It was outlined, written, and then rewritten. Then, the distractions came. But finally, with some help, Walker and Josie's story is now told. Thank you to Sue for the reading, Marybeth Renn for her eagle eye editing, and Joe Dugdale for the scrumptious cover. As always, my indulgent husband is my rock. And to you who are reading this, I appreciate you taking the time to read something I wrote. You are the best!

Praise for
Amazon #1 in Historical Romance and Romantic Suspense
&

USA TODAY BESTSELLING AUTHOR
ALYSSA BAILEY

What others are saying about Alyssa Bailey:

"Alyssa is an amazing author who captures the reader from the very beginning, holding them until the end and making them crave more. Can't wait for her next book!!!"

~ Bhanington reviewer for Booksprout "The O'Connors Series"

"This is the first book I've read by this author and I absolutely loved it. Has a great storyline that you can get right into from the very beginning and I got so engrossed with this book that I lost some sleep as I didn't want to miss anything at all. I especially liked and loved the characters in this book, they really made the story in my opinion... The author has done such a fantastic job with this book and I will definitely be coming back for future books in the future, especially this series. I would definitely recommend this book to everyone."

~ Carrie-Ann Amazon Reviewer "Safe and Secure Series"

"I love this series and couldn't put any of them down before the ending. Fabulous read!!!

~Sunny- reviewer for Booksprout "The O'Connors Series"

I loved this second book in the Clearwater ranch series. You don't need to have read book one to enjoy this book. Sawyer is in love with Camille. Unfortunately, circumstances worked against them and they were separated from each other. Camille comes back home with her children and they get back together. This is the epitome of an Alyssa Bailey book. There is a strong male character and there is an old-fashioned feel to their relationship. I loved this story and I can't wait for the next book. I give this an enthusiastic 5*.

~MR Amazon Reviewer

Chapter 1

Josephine Christina Silver Rodriguez watched the last employee leave for the day with bittersweet regret. Anger and regret mingled with her tears as she gazed around the empty space. She plopped into her chair harder than she'd intended. Fired again. Well, in all honesty, she had never been fired from any job, but her last two employers had found creative ways to terminate her employment. This one said, after reviewing the positions they currently had, the company eliminated the ones the board felt they could do without. Pure economics, Mr. Raines had promised her.

"I have procured one month's severance pay for you, and I promise you the best reference. I'm sorry, Ms. Rodriguez. You can work through the end of the week."

"I appreciate that, Mr. Raines."

But seeing as it was four in the afternoon on Friday, and she was off the clock at four-thirty, that was no concession. She doubted she could clean her desk out that quickly and here she was, pulling the final bits together as proof that clearing her desk took longer than thirty minutes.

Mr. Raines did not like confrontation. Josie loved it. But what she didn't enjoy was collaborating. Maybe Josie's quest for the thrill of engaging in a battle of wits was more intense than she first thought because she had worked for two prestigious corporations and had been terminated from both. The truth was that since childhood, Josie had always wanted control. She didn't like to rely on anyone else for a job that she was also tasked to do. You never knew if you could trust another to do their best and their less than great performance would reflect negatively on her.

The only person in adulthood that she'd ever allowed to have her back was Walker Knight, and now even he was gone. He'd resigned himself to the realization that she was too much work and she couldn't release her control enough to all him to Daddy her. Josie loved Walker. There was never any doubt about that. She loved his daddy techniques, but was it a love that would last? She didn't know if that was in her. Likely, love wasn't something she could do forever. Her childhood had broken that part of her emotional self.

"Josie, why are you taking your things out of your desk?" asked her now ex-co-worker, Shawna.

"Oh, I thought you'd gone home. I picked up these incredibly handy organizers this week, and I forgot to bring them in, so I thought I'd put everything together at home. Then I'll be ready for Monday. Saves time, and I don't have anything pressing to do this weekend."

"If it works out well, I'll see about getting some for myself," said Shawna. "My desk has become like a battleground. See you Monday."

Josie didn't lie if she could help it, so she answered the woman truthfully. She did have organizers at home, and she would use them. She would be ready for Monday, but she left out the important part. She would be job hunting come Monday.

"Have a good weekend." And a good life.

She watched the last person in the office leave before removing her things from the wall at her side of the room. Four women shared the large office that doubled as their projects room. Josie was known for her organizational skills and her attention to detail. When she arrived, Mr. Raines had a disaster in his office. Files and calendars were a jumble, his meetings were often late or forgotten, and his projects were beginning to go the way of his schedule. Josie fixed everything before it was apparent she didn't play well in the sandbox.

Walker Knight was her latest and last boyfriend. He tried to help her, but it never really took. They had tried being together several times, but she simply wanted to do things on her own, in her own way. Walker hadn't agreed and had pushed back. Something she loved. The spark that got her blood rushing.

"What are you talking about on your own? We're a couple. That means we do the tough stuff together."

"I'm trying."

"By doing things like changing your tire, at twilight, on the shoulder of a side road? No, ma'am, that isn't being safe or letting me get you help. It isn't even you calling the roadside service for help. I think there needs to be some incentive as an encouragement to keep yourself out of danger."

There was a thrill that raced through her nerve endings and slickened her sex, but there was no way she was going to admit to that. She knew what was coming after that flat tire story was told. He didn't disappoint. Walker did like he always did when she went too far. He pulled her over his knee and spanked some sense into her. Well, that was his goal, but it never changed her thinking for long. It was worth it though because the sex afterward was amazing.

Soon after she and Walker became exclusive, Josie learned she absolutely loved it when Walker spanked her on her pink sexy bits. A little spanking before sex was just an aphrodisiac. Not everyone understood how wet and hot it got her, so she didn't share the attraction to more than her two closest friends, but then, they were Walker's sisters-in-law. They got it.

Josie sighed as she gathered her two large bags and a small box in her hand and looked around. It was clean as a whistle. She headed out the door. Mr. Raines had terminated her with class, not so her last employer. The previous employer had asked her several times to have dinner with him.

"I'm in a relationship, and you're married," she had reminded him.

"Yes, that is true, so we won't bother our partners about any of this. It's just a little excitement on the side, okay?"

Josie had turned him down flat, using the old excuse of not wishing to mix business and private life. In her heart, she hadn't desired any man in her life outside of Walker. She wasn't sure she ever would love another, even though now, for a second time, she and Walker were no longer an "item." Maybe it was time to leave Austin. Dallas was a great place to live and work if you believed the advertisements.

After quitting Gentry World Investments, the best and worst job she'd ever had, and where she had first met Walker, Josie never seemed to fit in well enough in the corporate world or in her personal life as she had on the ranch. If she were honest, the ranch life suited Josie better. It was working for Piper Gentry, now Knight, that hadn't turned out well for her.

She missed the Knight men and the way they took care of each other and their women and their employees. The pay wasn't bad, either. Piper Gentry married the middle brother, Jackson Knight. Workaholic that Piper was, she now had it all; her family home and productive ranch, an indulgent and loving husband who was also a stern Daddy Dom, a daughter, and a company that had yet to slow its growth.

While there had been a rough patch in Josie and Piper's friendship when Josie terminated her employment with GWI, Piper, and her sister-in-law Camille, who had married the youngest Knight brother, Sawyer, were all good friends now. So good in fact, that when she was eating her way through a pint of Blue Bell butter pecan ice cream, she spilled her guts on their weekly Thursday conference call, otherwise known as an end of week de-stressor, their boost to finish the week and tackle the weekend.

"So, I got another good reference today."

Camille squealed. "Wow! That's great, except... why would they give you a reference when you work? Oh, no. Are you kidding me? Again?"

"Yep, great reference, but as I read the exit paperwork, every area was rated high except one."

Camille, the nurse, moaned. "Do I dare ask?"

"I'll read it to you. 'Ms. Rodriguez is extremely competent and can handle most situations admirably. However, she is not a good team player, as in, she does not ask for help. Ms. Rodriguez chooses to complete a project alone, even when others could contribute their efforts and quickly accomplish the task. The job is always done with excellent results, but it is not always timely due to her insistence at performing solo. She is well-liked by her co-workers, but simply won't ask for a collaborative effort when one is desired.'"

"So," said Piper, "you want to be the queen bee and the worker bees. Control issues. Jackson would say that about me. It's hard to work together on things you know you can do alone, but as they pointed out, it's important that you do it."

"No, that isn't it. Well, maybe a little. I'd love the help; I just don't know how to ask for it and if I can do it, why not just do it? Throwback from my childhood when my mom constantly asked everyone for help to raise her brood of kids. Everyone knew our business, and I felt pitied and was teased for most of my childhood. I refuse to be that person. I love my mom dearly, but she didn't see anything wrong in asking for whatever she needed before she even tried to fulfill her want list alone. I can't be like that, which often translates into not asking for help. Who am I kidding? I don't ask for anything. Ever."

Camille said, "But you'd ask us for help if you needed it, right? If you needed food or rent or something big like that?"

Josie sighed. "Probably not."

"Okay, but you would accept our help if we offered it." Camille qualified.

"Possibly."

Piper, who had said very little, asked, "So what's your next move?"

"Well, I received a month's severance pay, and I do have a healthy savings account, so I thought I'd look in Dallas."

"What?" Piper yelled.

"Josie, that isn't acceptable," Camille said.

Josie laughed. "Camille, I'm not one of your children."

"Well, you're acting like it. You don't cut and run at the first sign of a problem. What would Walker say if he knew you were trying to head for the hills, literally?"

"I'm not, and I doubt he would care."

Piper spoke softly. "Of course, he'd care, Josie. The man has worshiped you for over two years. I can't see Walker allowing it without a lot of talking, a few hot bottom sessions, and some intense loving."

"I wish, but that's not us anymore. Walker and I aren't seeing each other, so I thought it was a good time to, you know, try something new."

"Since when?" asked Camille.

"Since when... what?" asked Josie.

"Since when have you and Walker stopped seeing each other?"

"Oh, about a month ago. He just got busy, and I didn't call. He seems frustrated with me, as usual. He wants more, deserves more, but I'm honestly not sure I'm ever going to want a house and white picket fence, a husband, kids. You know, like you two have. I had too many siblings and not enough of anything else. I guess it's turned into a thing with me. Home was never a refuge like it is for most people."

"Okay, you have the children, and I'll raise them." Camille laughed, but sobered quickly. "Honestly, Josie, you two are great together. Do you want me to talk to Walker?"

"No. Maybe Walker and I weren't meant to be, or maybe we'll be like you and Sawyer and wait a handful of years. Or Piper and Jackson and wait a decade." Josie groaned at her own words. "It is possible we weren't made for walking the same path. Our journey is different."

"Have you been re-reading those self-help books?" asked Piper.

Josie laughed. "Not yet."

"Could I at least put in a good word now and then for you?" asked Camille.

"Sure, but if I'm not what Walker wants, I'll survive."

After losing her job and being so damned tired of living alone, Josie felt sad, real pity-party sad. And while she would survive, that wasn't the same thing as thriving. She was always in the best place ever when she was with Walker. Maybe she was too needy, but for once, Josie knew that wasn't the case. More than likely, she wasn't needy enough. Those Knight men wanted to be helpful, and when it came to their women, damn near demanded it. And when you had one Knight, you bought into the whole family of capable women and Daddy Doms.

Josie wondered if Walker would ever be an option for her, or had she taken advantage of his focused attention too much while not allowing him in her life enough, and not showing him what he meant to her? Maybe he had decided he'd hung around long enough waiting for Josie to figure out her life. Well, she still hadn't figured it out. Wasn't that telling?

Walker was the eldest Knight brother, still young but more than ready to start the next stage of his forever life with a wife. Josie was still digging in her heels, worried she would end up like her mother, with children and nothing else. Her mom loved her life. She enjoyed each man she created a new life with, and her bohemian lifestyle suited her. It just didn't suit the goal-driven Josie or her scientifically minded brother, Art. The others were either too young or like their mother, with not a care in the world.

Like Josie, Art had not found a spouse, but unlike her, he didn't feel the need to marry or procreate except when creating genetic material meant for regenerating traumatized tissue. That was all she remembered about the research her brother did and all she wanted to know. He was happy. That's what mattered to her. Maybe she was the only one who wasn't satisfied.

Piper chimed in. "Do you mind if I send your resumé to some of my contacts that almost require that you work alone? I think one of them might suit you better than a purely corporate environment. How do you feel about working from home?"

"Nothing weird?"

"Promise," said Piper.

"Sure, I'll tweak my resumé and send it to you this weekend. I'll consider anything that I can do and that pays enough for me to cover my bills and a little more. Now, enough about my unscheduled vacation. Tell me what you are expecting come spring in your neck of the woods."

Chapter 2

Walker Knight strode out of the horse barn for the last time today. He was glad he had enough hands to get him out of mucking stalls and riding the fence line. He'd spent his youth doing just that for little compensation because it was his father's ranch then, and he was his father's son. Enough said. But even though he was the boss now, by the end of the week, he was worn out. He rode some part of the ranch every morning. Then he spent the rest of the day balancing books, checking breeding schedules, talking to vendors, and any number of operating issues that he had to address for two successful ranches.

Walker had wanted to hire an assistant, but he'd held off hoping Josie would move in with him, and he'd offer her the job. She had proven she easily understood the comings and goings of the ranch, and he truly enjoyed her when she was working for Piper. Then the whole sabotage and assorted chaos happened on Gentry land, sending his girl running back to Austin.

Josie had confided to Jackson later that she hadn't left because of the craziness. She'd left because Walker was becoming too important to her. She wasn't ready for that type of relationship. The kind that ceded the leadership role, when push came to shove, in her private life, making her vulnerable.

And there was one other thing, the Knight men were Daddies that spanked. Walker wasn't heavy-handed. He'd only swatted Josie on a couple of occasions to get her attention like guys sometimes did, but when Jackson had told him that was why she left, he was ready to spank her perfectly round ass to a red-hot mess for keeping that secret from him.

"You can't keep things to yourself, like you don't like it when I swat you. I can't read minds." They found she liked his spanking hand just fine during sex, but she didn't like punishment. "But honestly, no one likes paying the piper when it's necessary."

"It's obvious you aren't clairvoyant, because if you were, you'd know it's not because I don't like it, it's because I like you doing it too much. Something must be wrong with me. People don't get anxious for sexy time because of it."

"The 'it' being a spanking, right?"

She had blushed. "Yes."

"Well, Sugar, you're wrong. It is all about making you want more sexy time. Spanking is all about the sensual way it makes you feel. If swats on the butt didn't ramp up your need to knock boots with me, then it wouldn't be worth the effort." She had felt better about her libido after that. "Now punishment is another story."

These last few weeks had told Walker that not only was Josie scared of commitment; she was also afraid of any forward advancement in their comfortable, friends with benefits arrangement. She didn't want to give over or even share the reins of her life at all. He would have to push Josie into realizing that she wanted more with him. Walker had wanted more with

Josie ever since he had seen her at Piper's house, looking for the ingredients to create dinner for everyone.

If his girl needed a push, he would push in a way that she'd feel the loss and want the stability of *them*. About a month ago, he had called and canceled his weekend trip to Austin, citing work issues, and asked her to call him later in the week if he didn't call her first.

Their weekends together had become routine for nearly a year, and now they would be disrupted. Walker hated it, but he had to shake his girl up. Josie had never called him back. Damn, it had backfired, and now they had less than before. It was his fault, and he didn't know how to fix it.

Maybe what he thought they had was a pipedream. Was it possible it had just been convenient for Josie to be with him, not the love connection he thought they had? Regardless, Piper had been after him to find an assistant, or let her find one. He would look at the qualifications he needed this weekend and then give the list to Piper so she could get him help. Josie would have been perfect, but he didn't think they would hook up again. Josie didn't want help to do anything, and Walker, being a gentleman, and a Daddy, couldn't help but offer and be irritated when he was rebuffed every time, even when it was obvious she wanted it.

He spoke with his brothers about it later that evening. "Man, my ass is dragging."

"That's what that dust was," said Sawyer. He teased his eldest brother. "I told Jackson that it looked like someone was dragging an ass."

Walker threw his hat at his youngest brother. "Shut up, moron. I'm too tired to whup your ass tonight. I'll catch ya in the morning."

Sawyer laughed. "You can try, old man. I keep up with three curtain climbers. You'd better be up pretty early in the morning to get a jump on me."

The three brothers sat for a while and discussed the week behind them and the one coming up. Early spring was a busy time of year, and while it was still cold out, they had to be ready. Walker had been four when Jackson was born. Then, four years later, Sawyer had made his appearance. Now, the only one who didn't have a family of his own was Walker. He sometimes envied his brothers, and then, sometimes, he didn't.

"Hell, and damnation," said six and a half-year-old Eli as he stomped into the den. He stopped dead in his tracks when he spied his daddy and two uncles.

"Son, I think you need to explain yourself," said Sawyer. "And thank the good Lord your mother isn't within hearing distance."

"Well, mama said I have to watch what Lily wants tonight or read a book. Cowboys don't read books, not when the Avengers are on."

"I'd check your facts on that one. Cowboys and ranchers read more than they watch television," said Uncle Jackson.

"And books are wa-a-y better than any cartoon," said Uncle Walker.

"Yeah, well, I'm just a kid, and I'll read later. I need to watch TV now."

All three men burst out laughing. "I get it," said Sawyer, who was the first to gain control. "I tell you what. If you don't want to watch Lily's program, and you're super good, I'll let you watch pro bull riding with us."

"Really? Do I get to ride a bull when I get older?"

"Why sur-"

"Sawyer Knight, if you say what I think you're about to say, you had better check your sleeping bag for holes. Remember the horses," said Camille as she stood in the doorway with her hands on her hips. Eli had gotten a new horse last fall, and he had demanded to sleep in the barn for a week to help the horse transition to his new home. Sawyer had been expected to keep him company.

Sawyer put his hand up. "Don't worry, baby. I'm not buying any bulls."

Eli's eyes widened. "We can *buy* a bull?"

"No, son, that's Uncle Jackson's side of the ranch," said Sawyer as he watched his son climb onto Jackson's lap and begin asking all kinds of questions.

"My work here is done," smiled Camille as she sauntered past the men.

Walker fiddled with the remote while he asked Piper as she passed the group, "How was your chat with Josie?"

"Good, there is so much going on."

Walker sat straighter in the recliner. "Everything all right?"

"Well, it could be better, but she's fine. Better than I'd be. She's decided to move to Dallas."

Walker's words were more demanding. "Dallas? Dammit. What's going on? "

"Oh, you know, she got this excellent recommendation, so she decided to take it to Dallas."

"The hell she is. Wait, recommendation, meaning she lost her job again?"

"I didn't say that, Walker."

"Uncle Walker, that's two bad words you've said. Mama is gonna make you put money in the swear jar. There are ladies in the room," said Eli in his most proper, chastising voice.

The adults again broke out into laughter, and the moment was over. Walker needed to find out what was really going on. He'd corner Camille later. She had a soft spot for romance.

IT HAD BEEN TWO WEEKS since Josie had lost her job, and except for a few first interviews, nothing had panned out. She'd landed her last position in a week and the one before that she had gotten before leaving GWI. It was now Thursday again, and time to swallow some pride and ask Piper if any of her contacts had responded. Josie tried not to think of it as asking for help, but her worry button had been pushed, and if it went on for another two weeks, her panic button would get punched. She hadn't touched her savings yet, but that day was in the foreseeable future.

"Hey, Josie, how's the job hunt?" asked Camille.

Josie sighed dramatically. "Nothing so far. I would usually have one by now."

"Don't worry, you will. It takes a little time," said Piper.

"Well, how about your contacts, Piper?"

"Yes, actually. Someone I admire a great deal, a good employer, and very hands-on in the running of the corporation has just sent over a request to see if I know of anyone who might fit the bill. He needs an assistant. But like I said, he is hands on, and any assistant he has will need to be as well."

"What does he do?"

"He likes to say he is the overseer, but actually, he's an administrator that touches base with his employees daily."

"So, what's the business?"

"Clearwater-Knight Enterprises, which is Clearwater Gentry and Clear Knight Ranches. It also includes GWI and Gentry Real Estate, but Walker just handles the ranches. We all have a vote on everything, though."

"Oh, no. I'm not going to be Walker's assistant when we don't even see each other anymore, which was his decision."

"Didn't he leave the ball in your court, and you never called him?" asked Camille. "Josie, he misses you."

"That man has a funny way of showing it. No, Piper."

"Walker really is looking for an assistant," said Piper.

"Wonderful. I hope he finds one, but it won't be me."

"But you'd be perfect!" chimed in Camille. "I'm not sure you won't get paddled at work if you don't follow the rules, though. That's the downfall of working at home near Sawyer. It's harder to get away with things. On the flip side, I get more daytime cuddles. I'm positive Walker really thought you'd call. Maybe he thinks you don't want a relationship with him. I could..."

Josie was adamant. "No. Besides, he won't want me to be his assistant."

Camille spoke. "Not true, Josie. He's always asking me after our phone call if you're all right. If you've found a job. Is there anything he needs to do for you? I tell him you're fine and all, but it seems like he's looking to do something for you. He muttered something about you needing a good spanking to relax you and help you see things his way, but I told him that would not be a selling point for you."

Josie tried to ignore her clenching buttocks, her tingling lower belly, and dancing core. She desperately needed relief and a good romp between the sheets. "He hardly ever swatted me, so I think he was joking."

Except before sex, during sex, even a little after sex. Her lady bits were weeping just remembering his hand on her ass, then dipping between her lower lips, running along her slit and then taking the honey with him to invade her dark entrance and... What had they been talking about?

Silence reigned for what seemed like long minutes. Piper spoke. "Um, I'm not so sure our Knight men tease about that. But if you aren't going to take the job, then I guess it won't matter whether he is serious or not, right?"

Josie agreed and wondered why she felt so sad about it. "Right."

Her voice held less enthusiasm than she would have hoped.

"Okay, but Piper, can you hold the job for another week just in case Josie doesn't get something? I mean, what's an occasional sexy spanking in comparison to a good job? It's nothing, and it could be fun," said Camille.

"That's what you think," murmured Josie.

"What?" asked Camille.

"Nothing. Don't worry. I'll get something this week, I'm sure. Can we change the subject?"

If they stayed on this subject, Josie would be crying and she had decided she wasn't going to cry over this. She was going to put on her big girl panties and find a job herself. Then her mind wandered to the cute pony panties he had bought her and the kitten ones, then the puppy ones. She loved them. And that was the way to start crying. Memories sucked. And being without Walker sucked worse.

Chapter 3

Walker strode into the offices of Gentry Worldwide Investments and waved at the receptionist. Piper's office in town had grown from a satellite office to handle executive meetings and her day-to-day investment work, to include a satellite office for the ranches and her real estate holdings. All the businesses were now held under the larger corporate umbrella of Clearwater-Knight Enterprises. To say that the specialty livestock businesses were more than profitable would be an understatement.

Walker had taken Sawyer's suggestion and started looking for another property to make his own. Sawyer had the most children and the horses, which were already doing well on the Knight homestead. Jackson had all but moved the entire cattle operation to Piper's property, now owned by the corporation as well. Walker thought Josie would have liked her own home, but it didn't matter now. She was moving further away from him. But he was still in search of a property, and he may have found one. The Martin Place. It was priced too high last time he checked, but the woman he had interviewed recently, against his better judgment, for the assistant job, seemed pretty interested in taking the job. It was worth another look at both the prospective employee and the property. He had been biding his time. He hoped Piper could get him more information.

Piper was in her element in the office and a kickass wife and mother when at home. She said one child was probably enough for them, but Jackson kept his own counsel for now. He'd alluded to his brothers that he would like one more but understood that he or she would need to come with a nanny. He was sitting with that reality. When Josie and Walker's relationship was closer, the subject of children had come up. He recalled the conversation.

Walker brought the subject up. "Piper thinks she may only want their one, but Camille would probably have ten if Sawyer didn't say they had all they could deal with right now. I know I want one, and I can't imagine not having any, but ten might be pushing it." He laughed. "How about you?"

"I'd like one, but I don't know about two." Josie had given her reason. "They're so expensive, and I'm not going to be put in the same position as my mother, having so many children and asking for handouts."

"Baby, you would never have to ask for a handout. We make enough money. Hell, you wouldn't have to work."

Josie shook her head. "No, I'm never relying on someone else for my income. I've seen what it does to people."

"It makes them vulnerable, and I know that bothers you. But I want you to understand that you would never be dependent on another to live." He scrubbed his hands over his face, realizing it was an ongoing battle or Josie to allow anyone in too far. "Fine, then work at the ranch and throw your income into savings for a rainy day. You'd have a family, a job, and me." Walker thought that was a perfect solution.

"Maybe, if I can lower my worry enough to have children."

He knew she loved kids, was good with his nieces and nephews, so Walker, like his brother, had wisely kept his own counsel. Her growing up was traumatic for her. He could wait it out some.

Walker sat in one of the two chairs in front of Piper's desk, prepared to wait her out. Piper, chatting on the phone, held up one finger to indicate she'd be another minute. When he nodded agreement, she pointed to her coffee carafe in the corner. He moved his finger between her and the pot, silently asking if she wanted a cup. She shook her head. He nodded and got up to fill a cup for himself. He and headstrong Piper didn't always get along, but he loved his sister-in-law, who had been like a little sister since she was two years old.

He looked up when Piper hung up and smiled at his overachieving sister before asking, "How are you holding up today?"

"I'm trying to finish this real estate deal, but the seller is cantankerous." She pushed the papers spread out on the desk into a folder and set it to the side. "Now, what brings my favorite brother-in-law to see me in town instead of at the ranch?"

"Your favorite, huh? Should we tell Sawyer?" he grinned when she shook her head. "A couple of things. I was in town on business, so I thought I'd stop and see how the hunt for my assistant was coming. It's been nearly two weeks, Piper. I know you work faster than that."

"I do. I'll have an answer for you by Friday."

"Who is it?"

"Is it okay if the assistant is a woman? I mean, those are the ones that have worked best for me."

"I don't mind if she can do the things on that list. Do cattle inventory with a tag scanner? Understand auctions? Willing to live on the ranch or maybe in one of your duplexes? I need her to be close. What are her credentials?"

"I can have her on the ranch as a requirement for the first six months if that's okay. After that, she can go anywhere she wants that will allow her to get to work on time. Listen to her education: BA in Business Management, master's in business-Corporate, and several endorsements. I've spoken to her past employers, and they have nothing but good things to say about her."

"Why isn't she still working for them?"

"Downsizing."

"Yeah, that can be tough. But if she was good..."

"One of those last in, first out situations."

He nodded. "Right. Well, what's her name?"

"Um, I wrote it down somewhere. Tina, I think. Tina Gold."

"Where is she from originally?"

"Tell you what, I have her references being checked, but I can email you her resumé as soon as Remy is done with it, okay?"

"Yeah, that would be good. Unlike temp cowboys, I'd like to meet her before I sign her on."

"Of course. I'll send everything over to you, and then you can decide. I've already interviewed her and think she'd be a great asset. I think if you don't snatch her up, I will."

"Alrighty then, send her info over, and I'll look. The other thing is the Old Martin Place."

"Is it up for sale again?" Piper perked up. "I didn't get that information."

The Martins, now only Branch Martin, owned a good piece of land adjacent to the corner where Knight and Gentry land met. It would be a feather in their cap if they could get it. Especially if Walker built his house there.

"Well, not quite. Branch was talking to me a few days ago and mentioned he thought he would rather just put it up for sale. The upkeep was more than he would ever do."

"Okay, I'll send over some information this week sometime."

"Thanks. See ya later." Walker stood and dropped a kiss on his sister-in-law's cheek before leaving.

As Walker headed toward the feed store, he felt less relieved than he expected about the prospect of getting the help he so desperately needed. He wondered what was up with him. It was past time that he got an assistant. He told himself that it was apparent Josie wasn't interested in being with him, let alone working for him, so he had to look elsewhere. Who knew, maybe this new woman was a looker. He might have gotten excited if he thought it would matter, but it didn't. He loved Josie.

Walker stopped in his tracks when he realized two things: he had no desire to look past Josie to fill his off-hours, and this woman might be married and need to go home every night. She'd have to live near, or she wouldn't have applied, surely. He'd wait until he got the email from Piper before assuming anything. And he'd give more thought to making a trip to Austin to set a too self-sufficient little girl straight.

WALKER WOULD READ THROUGH the rhizome that came through email after dinner. The women were having their Thursday night chat with Josie, and if she didn't have a job, he wondered why they continued in the weekly routine. They could have called anytime. Camille, the quieter of the two Knight women, said habits were hard to re-establish after broken.

"Besides," Camille said at the dinner table, "when she moves to Dallas, there won't be any chance to talk much until she gets a place and a job."

"She's not moving to Dallas," grumbled Walker.

"Whatever you want to tell yourself, brother dear, but she has begun to pack up. She has had several interviews set for late next week. She figures if she can get there by then, and if it works out, she'll stay since her lease is up next month. It works out really well, actually." Camille gave her son more mashed potatoes and left the discussion to continue in Walker's head.

Suddenly, he didn't have an appetite and encouraged the conversation to move on to other ranching subjects. Walker soon fell weary of the ranching report from Sawyer and excused himself, saying he had work to do. He did. There was a never-ending pile of work to plow through, but he thought he would take a quick look at the resumé while he considered what to do to keep Josie close. Dallas was too damn far. He could get to Austin in an hour if he had to, but Dallas was well over three. If she needed help, he didn't have any friends living there to get her the help she needed fast.

No, he wasn't ready for Josie to leave, so he'd have to work something out with Piper, maybe trick his girl into staying. Piper could offer her a job working in Austin, not working with Piper, which had proven to be a bad idea a few years ago. Yes, that would work. With that issue settled in his mind, Walker pulled up the email and looked at the applicant.

Tina Gold, why did that sound slightly familiar? He didn't know any Golds, but the full name... never mind, he told himself, it's the credentials and experience he was looking to hire, not her name. Huh, this girl gave a box number so you couldn't find her to harass. Good girl. If this were true, the woman had impressive work experience, excellent credentials, and the extra sheet attached said her references all checked out.

Her past employers included a couple of smaller ranches some time ago and several corporate businesses. Piper had done an excellent job screening the applicant who said she wasn't married and could relocate. It didn't matter if she was married, but most women didn't move the family, so he had assumed she would be single or live close already. This Tina said she rode and liked the rodeo. Josie loved the rodeo. This applicant would be a dream if he weren't already hopelessly in love with Josie.

Walker reached across the desk for his phone and knocked over his favorite picture of him and Josie. He knew he was pathetic, but he wasn't ready to let go. Maybe Ms. Tina Gold would be able to help him with his problem at work and personally.

"Piper? I want to meet her and hire her."

"Yeah? Good, I thought you might. Let me put this tired little munchkin in bed, and I'll set up a time."

"Perfect. I'm open tomorrow."

JOSIE WONDERED WHY Piper was so excited. Camille was trying to be polite. Too polite.

"Something wrong, Cami?" asked Josie.

"No, sorry, but Sawyer just discussed his annoyance with me last night about getting into other people's business, so I'm trying hard to practice staying out. He's right about other people, but you two are different. Men don't seem to understand. I do want to know what's going on, Piper."

"You can be nosy on these calls. It's a naughty free zone," said Josie. "Now spill, Piper."

"Oh, um, just business, nothing to worry about. Looking at purchasing the old Martin place that butts up to our ranched to the west. It's a good buy if we can get it. Walker wants to build on it if we get it. Anyway, so Josie, how's the job hunt?"

"Thanks, Piper," Josie answered with sarcasm. "I was in a good mood until that question. The Martin place is a beautiful bit of land. Walker has always wanted it."

"Well, if all goes well, he will finally have it. Now don't avoid the subject. Job prospects?"

"Maybe in Dallas."

Camille sighed. "Still no luck? I'm sorry. It's been a month. Maybe Piper has a lead. I guess you could wait tables. I remember the tips being good. It paid for my extras because, after daycare and nursing school, I rarely had more than enough to buy food and pay rent. Sometimes not even that. When I could pull a couple of shifts a week at the restaurant, I made about 500 dollars. I was exhausted, but it got us through."

"Wow, that's a lot of tips. Anyway, I have to spill the beans. No need to wait tables because I have a job offer for you! And I waitressed in college too. Not what a business major should be doing, though. What I have here is much better."

"Less about you and more about me, please. Tell me," demanded Josie.

"I have the authority to offer you a job as an executive assistant. Do you want me to send you over the proposed offer?"

"Absolutely. That would be awesome. How much does it pay?"

"Forty thousand to start. It also provides room and board."

"What? That's incredible. What's the catch?"

"Yes, well, there is one. You have to realize the room and board are near your place of business because your prospective employer needs you to be close. He isn't too demanding, but he is a stickler for punctuality."

"Sounds like Walker. He never pushed me to do things or not do them, well, not unless they were for the standards, health and safety, but man, if you were late without a good reason. Whew. And if I made him late without cause, well, let's just say, one of the few times he swatted my ass for a real reason was that. I made him wait for an hour, and my phone was off. Anyway, let's not talk about Walker anymore, tell me about this boss. Is he handsome? No, wait, is he married?"

"Why? Does that matter?"

"I guess not, but if he is handsome and married, then his wife will hate me. If he is good looking and single, no problem except maybe he would think he got extra privileges."

"Well, he isn't like that, but handsome, yes, married, no. You don't have to worry about things because he only has eyes for one woman. Save the rest of your questions until I send the info over. Then ask."

"That's fair."

"And if you agree, he'd like to meet you tomorrow to start work on Monday. He'll give you a week to move in, so this weekend through next weekend. I have a trailer we can loan you to transport your household items."

"Wow, okay, get me the information. Thanks Piper. I didn't want to ask, but I was desperate. See, maybe I am getting better asking for help."

Piper snorted. "Yeah, after we waited a month and prodded you at every turn."

Camille asked, "Piper, what about Walker? Did he ever find a person?"

"Yeah, he did. Her name is Tina."

"Oh, that's a nice name. I'm excited to meet her," said Camille.

"We all are," agreed Piper.

Josie remained silent. Suddenly, her new job had lost its appeal. All Josie could think about now was who this Tina woman was. How old was she, was she married, and if not, did she expect to stay at the ranch with Josie's man? Okay, maybe he wasn't her man right now, but dammit, she had worked hard to get him the way she liked him, giving in to her whims, and no woman was going to hijack him right from under her nose.

And what did Walker think he was doing, hiring some young chick as his assistant? She probably didn't know the first thing about keeping the books for a ranch. Two ranches now. Two ranches that had world renowned breeding stock horses and prime herds of cattle. This Tina wouldn't know the first thing about keeping stock numbers and inventory of the feed, price checking, and what about counting and tagging? Then there were the Knight men's quirks.

Did she understand the number system, what was expected? Jackson, Sawyer, and Walker could get awfully upset if their systems were tampered with in any way. It would be their reputation if any of that were mixed up. She couldn't imagine the flames coming from Jackson Knight if he found out his breeding was contaminated for a whole season. And if Sawyer's horses were becoming world renowned, no, that simply wouldn't do. This woman had no idea what Walker was like when he was stressed and needed to be left alone completely for a time.

Walker didn't know what this woman was capable of either. Just what was he thinking? General office work, like customer accounts and the like, sure, but Josie had helped Walker put that filing system in place, and the idiosyncrasies were because Walker's brain worked differently than most and what most would consider correct filing, didn't work for Walker. She remembered when she had discovered he didn't look for customer files by name, but by the animal sold to them. No, Walker had no idea what he was getting himself into with this unfamiliar woman.

FOR THE SECOND DAY in a row, Walker strode into the local GWI offices in search of Piper. Yesterday he was in town so he just said hello. Not today. He stopped as the office door opened, but his sister wasn't as observant as he. She barreled into his hard chest.

"You could have moved out of the way, Walker. You Knight men are such great oafs sometimes. What are you doing here, anyway?"

Walker considered her for a moment. Jackson called his wife feisty. In this mood, Walker called her something else. "I wondered if we could postpone the meeting with Tina until Monday. I had to come to get a couple of things Jackson needed, so I thought I'd stop by instead of calling. I should help Jackson with the cattle today. He's trying to breed the new bull, but not having much luck. I used to be pretty good at enticing the ladies." He laughed at his own joke.

"Huh, and yet you're single."

"Not of my choosing, brat. Does my brother know how snarky you are in the morning? Do you need a spanking to get it all out?"

"No thank you. We discuss it often, now if you want me to handle it, I can. You can get on with the cow calls or whatever, but your candidate, sorry, your new employee needs to be able to start moving in this weekend. Otherwise, she can't start for another couple of weeks."

"Damn. I forgot about that. I'm so backlogged now, every week we wait makes my life that much more difficult." Walker ran his hand up and down the short hairs on the back of his head. "Fine. Let's do it. I trust your judgment. Think she'll want us to clean up the foreman's cabin? Since Cody hooked up with Jasmine, it's been empty. I can get Camille to pull in a few teens to clean it up."

"Oh, that hadn't occurred to me. I thought you'd just throw Tina into the main house in the far bedroom, but you might be right. She'd like her own space. Less awkward for her."

"And me," said Walker.

"It's set then. I'll call Camille and get that part going."

"I'd try the new barn first. We had a foal last night, and you know Camille; there aren't enough children, family, or workers for her to get her doctoring out. She cuddles every new animal on both ranches."

"She's just the nurturing kind, and let's face it, with me as the other woman in the family, she needed to be."

Walker chuckled. "You're right about that."

"Okay, I have things to do. Did I tell you that Josie got a job yesterday?"

"She did? In Dallas?" He wasn't happy about that, but he could understand that she needed to make a living. If it had to be in Dallas, well then, it did.

"Nope. But she is moving out of her apartment, so she doesn't have to drive so far every day. She's happy to finally have gotten one without a bigger move."

"That's good. Tell Josie I hope she enjoys the new job. And if she needs some help, she can always ask. It wouldn't take but a few hours to have things moved. That girl refuses to buy anything that isn't absolutely necessary. She wouldn't let me gift her much either."

"I'll tell her. You know she won't ask for help, she will figure it out herself. And you remember her background was rough, so she never wants to spend money."

"I remember only too well. You tell that girl that I still have paddling rights if she moves anything heavy."

Piper rolled her eyes. "I will not."

Walker dropped a kiss on his sister-in-law's head before opening the door and heading down the street. While he was glad Josie had gotten a job, he wasn't as happy about her moving to a place he hadn't vetted yet. It'd taken him a while to convince her on that first apartment after she had left GWI, that just because it cost a few dollars less, forty to be exact, she shouldn't compromise her safety for it. He had put his foot down, and so had Josie. They added a bolt for the door, and she had moved to a safer location when the lease was up. That seemed to be the way they compromised.

He knew she wouldn't ask for help, and that was one of the reasons they'd had several loud conversations. On her last move, Walker had gotten a call from an emergency room clerk saying Josie needed someone to drive her home after her leg was cast. That had done it. When he arrived, he found out the whole story. She'd tried to move her bedroom set, her four-poster, solid oak bedroom set, alone.

The large dresser had hit a snag. It jerked the mirror that evidently had been poorly attached, and Josie had chosen not to remove first. The mirror teetered. Josie, trying to save the antique piece, dove over an armchair in the middle of the floor. She landed on the chair, and the mirror promptly fell on her, shattering. She was in the emergency room with a busted leg and some cuts and bruises. She lamented the loss of her mirror.

Walker's hand itched for days after that escapade, but once she had settled into the cast, he had expressed his thoughts concerning her putting herself at risk rather than asking for help, all over her butt. She was understandably irritated at first. Josie got off on his hand bouncing off her ass in sex or just prior to some sexy time, but this had not been about that. It had been about the fact that he was falling in love with her, and the thought of what could have happened, all because of her stubbornness, was unbearable.

"Josie, it's not weak to ask for help, it actually shows intelligence. It says you have assessed the situation, factored in that you are not Wonder Woman, and chose to go with being safe. This time you broke your leg, next time, who knows?"

Between swats and screeches of outrage, Josie had yelled, "Are you saying I am unintelligent, Walker Knight?"

"Nope, I'm saying you don't use your brains when you should. The very next time we have this conversation, I will strip you bare, and you will dance to the tune of my belt. You got me?"

"Yes, dammit. You know I don't like to ask for help. It makes me vulnerable. Old habits die hard. I don't know why the hell it matters now. I already broke my leg."

That was the wrong thing to say to a lover trying to get his safety lesson across. Another flurry of swats landed on Josie's upturned ass.

"I don't have the urge to go all cowboy on you often, but when I do, you know it's for something big. When you find yourself over my lap, or in this case, on your belly, on the bed, I'm in control. And because you put yourself in harm's way for no good reason, you had better be calling me sir instead of cursing me. Your past isn't an excuse to put yourself in risky situations now. You could have asked me. Allowing me to help you should never make you feel vulnerable."

"And yet, it does, *Sir*. Ouch."

Josie had disclosed to him during a drowsy afterglow of flaming hot sex, that she loved it when he made her call him "sir" in the bedroom. If he slid an inquiring finger below, he'd find her hot and slick after every spanking. Outside of their private space and lovemaking, Walker knew her well enough not to attempt the move. But he had few times that it was a challenge to wait until they were in a private setting.

Josie kicked her one good leg, the other was healed, but the cast was not yet removed. Walker grinned, confident she couldn't see him. He sure liked to hear her call him "sir" when he was irritated. Even when she was snarky about it, Walker knew she loved their little slap and tickle, but this was serious.

"Please, Walker, can we be done?"

"We'll be done when I think you *have* gotten the message because I'm here to tell you this is going to stop. Hear me?" He scooted closer. His hand bounced off her cute little butt so well and felt so good that he'd swelled to an uncomfortable size. It was evident he wasn't the only one who noticed when Josie had slipped her closest hand down, accurately landing on his lap and rubbing the discomfort. He tried to rearrange her and finally held her hand. The little minx. Evidently, she wanted spanking time to be over. He landed another swat.

"Yes, Sir. Please, honey, I know what you're saying makes sense. I just can't be like my mom. You know that."

Walker did stop then. Pulling her carefully onto his lap, her cast maneuvering awkwardly, he scooted them back against the headboard of the enormous, now moved, bed. Walker held her tight, his chin resting on top of her head. His hand smoothed her hair.

"I know sugar. It's hard for most people to ask for help, but we do. And you should have no problem asking me for help. It scares me when I can't trust you'll put your safety first."

"I'll try harder."

Walker was aware that there had been some improvements, but he knew it wasn't enough for him to not be concerned that she'd end up in the same situation again. Back then, she wouldn't even talk to him about her needs or ask for help. She would have called a cab rather than let the hospital contact him. Although his girl still had a lot of progress to make, he expected they'd have similar conversations in the future. However, things remained unchanged since then.

It was a different time now; no longer did Walker feel like his and Josie's paths were entwined. He still loved her, even though they had broken up, and he wanted to make things better for her if only she would let him. But he knew deep down that he had to try to move on; even though it felt impossible, he knew Josie could survive without him as she had before they met.

The new hire looked good on paper, but the spark of hope in his heart was fading concerning Josie. Could this new person really turn his life around, lessen his worry and job strain giving him the time and renewed connection he longed for? Would it give him the chance to bring him back to the love and joy he had with Josie? And even if he and the new assistant hit it off better than he was anticipating he wanted. It was hard to move on, but could he even contemplate that eventuality? Could he forget Josie completely? He wasn't sure he was ready for a change.

Chapter 4

Josie was worried. She'd had lunch with Piper and Camille. Camille had patients that afternoon, and while Josie needed Camille's upbeat personality, she also wanted to talk to Piper alone. So she was relieved when Camille left to work.

"Piper, what's going on?"

"Okay, so I wasn't exactly truthful."

"What? So, there is no job, right?" Josie had been apprehensive but determined to try to work for someone she had never met. Large operations did that all the time.

"Oh, no, there is definitely a job. And the employer wants to hire you. In fact, I was given the go-ahead to do just that if I thought you would work out."

"And do you?"

"Yes." Piper smoothed out her used paper napkin. She stirred the lemon in her water.

"Okay, so what's the *but*?"

"There is none. Why are you always so suspicious?"

"I know you. And when you fiddle with your napkin, water, plate, and everything else, it's because you don't want to say something you should."

Piper sighed. "It's just that you have to live local to the job."

"And…" Josie gave her friend a look that said she didn't buy the story Piper was trying to sell.

"And nothing. I knew you wanted to stay close, and I have properties to lease, so we would both be winning because you get a stipend if you live in town. I'd recommend in town rather than on-site."

"Why?" Josie's radar was still beeping.

"Because you're going to want a space of your own when not working. You got that email I sent you, the one from Wal...Walt? Walt." Piper mentally kicked herself in the butt. She almost ruined everything.

"Yeah, Walt seems genuinely nice, on paper anyway."

"He is. A little rough around the edges but a hard worker, and he could use your help. He's been looking and waiting for the right person. He's been waiting for you. But you know ranchers, you'd never get a break from the office or the work if you lived on the ranch."

"Oh, so he's like you and all three of the Knight men? Yeah, I'd probably be better in town. Do you have time to show me what you have available?"

"Not really, but I do have the keys. First, you need to sign the paperwork."

"Okay, I trust your judgment. I wouldn't have accepted a job with an employer that I don't know and haven't met otherwise. He must trust you too, not to need the interview."

"I really like him, and I think you will too. I forgot to ask if you can do the payroll, or do I need to offer one of my people to do it?"

"I can do it, but who was doing the man's payroll before now?"

"He pays for it to be done or rather, the ranch does. Anyway, it would just be easier if he could have it done in house. He tends to like to outsource as little as possible."

"A control freak, huh?"

"Nope, just a man who likes to see all the operations if he needs to do something or change things up a bit. Most ranchers, big and small, like that."

"Walker was like that. You were like that."

Piper laughed. "I can tell you firsthand, he still is, and so am I, but he's learned how to run two ranches pretty well."

"Did you say he hired an assistant too?"

"He hired the day before this job came available. You know, he wanted you." Piper said with conviction.

"What?"

"That man held the job open for you, hoping you would want it."

"Well, I do have a lot of experience with ranches, and especially yours."

"Yeah, but he runs both, most days. I just do the little part we agreed to, and he does the rest. I run the numbers after he does to make sure we don't miss anything."

"And does he?"

"Nope." Piper shoved the contract paperwork towards Josie. Josie began signing where Piper pointed. As soon as the last signature was in place, Piper scooped up the papers.

"I'll get you a copy of all this Monday, okay? Stop by the office Monday at 8:00 a.m. I'll have the copies and your directions to your new job. Start moving into the duplex you want, and I'll get that paperwork done for Monday, too." Piper looked at her phone. "I'm late, gotta go. You'll probably want to get home and finish packing."

"Yeah, I need to be out in ten days," said Josie, who looked a little shell-shocked.

"Need help?"

"Funny."

"Well, I do know you will need help to move your things out, especially that bedroom set. Want me to send the guys over on Sunday to do that?"

"I don't want..."

"To ask, I know. But I *did* ask, and I *am* sending people over there. Sunday after lunch. They will bring a trailer and enough guys to get you out of there in an hour, two tops."

"Thanks. That would help."

"Okay, see you Sunday afternoon or Monday for sure."

Piper was out the door without a backward glance. Things just seemed off. Josie couldn't get rid of the feeling that Piper was up to something. Josie knew what Jackson thought of his wife putting her nose into places it didn't belong. Josie chuckled. "That girl is going to find sitting a whole new experience if she's causing trouble."

Piper had told Josie once that Jackson's take-charge attitude when they were at home, did it for her. She still ran an incredibly dynamic corporation, but when she was home, she liked him to handle things. He did too. Josie remembered when she worked for Piper and was stationed at the ranch. She had fought him tooth and nail for control. They finally compromised, and from where Josie stood, it was making them both happy.

Josie couldn't help but think about what it would be like to work with Walker. Now she would never know. Josie had to admit that the other woman, Tina, was lucky to be on the ranch with those men. She would come under their protection, and that was pretty special. She wondered if his new assistant was single. That hurt her heart to think that there was a possibility someone else was going to snag Walker Knight instead of Josie. She knew that she hadn't done the right thing by him. He had wanted a relationship, and honestly, so did she, but he'd done all the compromising. She did all the mulish behavior.

Now that she was moving close, really close, Josie wondered if Walker would be willing to try again. She would do better at letting him into her life. She also knew that Walker had standards and a way of life that she was afraid to try. She had pushed, and he had pushed back. Josie had demanded to be allowed to do everything herself, and Walker had wanted to help her with everything. Worse, he would do it himself if she'd let him, and that just wasn't what she was comfortable with, not after growing up in the environment she had.

Josie thought that it was unreasonable for Walker to expect her to give over her control so that he could have it. Yes, sometimes it didn't work out for her, and she got hurt physically, or she didn't finish early at work, or she even missed out on opportunities because she couldn't ask to join in things. Walker said it was a real problem she needed help with. If Josie couldn't ask for someone to pick her up a coke, how was she going to have someone work with her and her control issues and her feelings of inadequacy? Walker had said it was unhealthy. He wanted to work with her on pushing past her hesitancy, but it had turned into a holy mess.

"Anytime you want to try to get past this thing you have about asking for help," he'd told her, "then you just pick up that phone, sugar. Until then, I'm not sure we can go further. The ball is in your court."

Suddenly, he had more important work and had said it would be spring at the ranches before they knew it, but Josie had no doubt it was her lack of sharing herself with him. He was right. She was broken, and likely irreparable. That was two months ago. Maybe she could try again if it wasn't too late.

MONDAY MORNING, RIGHT on time, Josie walked into Piper's office and was surprised to find only her office manager and an assistant. "Is Piper running late?"

"Running late? I didn't know she was coming in this morning."

"Well, she's supposed to take me out to the ranch for my new job, or at least my paperwork and the directions, so I guess she scheduled herself off."

"Maybe, but... I'll just give her a call."

As the young lady was putting in the call, Josie stepped into the bathroom to make sure she looked presentable and, because when she was nervous she had to pee, or at least she had that burning urgency. She rarely actually needed to go, but you couldn't be sure. As soon as Josie relaxed, it would go away. She walked out and noticed Piper's door was now closed.

Josie pointed to the office. "Is Piper in?"

"No, that's her brother-in-law. Now..."

"Did you get in touch with her?"

"No," said the manager with a frown, "But..."

"Okay, well, can you call the employer and get the exact address. I'll use my phone to get there."

"But why don't you..."

"Really, this will work out fine."

The confused manager nodded. "I'll just call him and get that information for you." The manager handed a packet of paper to her. "This is probably the paperwork you were expecting. The rental agreement isn't completed yet. Do you mind waiting?"

"No, so long as you know I am moving in."

"Fine. Do you have the other duplex key?"

"Yes." She pulled out a key from her jeans pocket and gave it to the woman.

Josie wished she could see into Piper's office because then she could see which Knight was in there, Walker or Sawyer. She sat in one of the plush waiting room chairs and opened the packet to read while she waited.

As the call was going through, Josie marveled at how a woman who ran a diverse corporation could forget her appointment. She scanned the front page when something caught her eye. She re-read it. "Josephine, aka Josie Rodriguez, contracts to work for Clearwater-Knight enterprises. as a personal assistant to Walker Knight, Owner."

A feeling of sick dread engulfed Josie, and as she leaned back in her chair to process what this meant, Walker jerked open the door and angrily strode out, only glancing at Josie as he made a beeline to the office manager.

"What the hell is this?" Before the woman could answer, he turned on Josie. "Were you in on this?"

"What? In on what? You mean that we have both been duped into accepting and offering jobs to people that didn't exist?"

Walker stared for a moment before he calmed down. Giving her a frustrated frown and a shake of his head, he said, "No, sugar, this was all Piper Kay, and I am going to make sure she remembers this little fiasco for a long time." Walker sat down in the seat next to Josie, hard enough to make the soft chair groan. "Sorry, I lost my temper. It never helps." He ran his hand over the back of his neck. "What are we going to do?"

"I'm not sure what I can do. Piper has made a huge problem for me. I gave up my apartment, and she offered this duplex, but if I don't have a job, then I can't afford even the lowered rent."

"Oh, don't you worry, you'll have a place to be. Let's get out of here because if I see my sister-in-law before I have things worked out, and you settled, I'll grab the nearest implement and spank her ass until it's glowing as I share my irritation over her methods of manipulation. Then I'll turn her over to her husband. That would not be a good choice for either of us." Walker stood and put out his hand. "Come on, baby, you look like you've just returned from the war. We'll figure this out, promise."

Baby. She loved it when he called her that. It meant she was cherished. And someone who needed his help, which she didn't. Except she did, dammit. Josie snapped out of her stupor. "No, I can figure things out. It's just going to take me a little time."

"Josie, darlin', *we* are figuring this out. Have you had breakfast?"

"I had coffee. I shouldn't spend the money until I know what I'm doing."

Walker slid his hand down to the small of her back like it belonged there. It was muscle memory or something like that and she loved it. He gently propelled her forward.

"So, no. I could always eat." He turned back and told the woman at the desk, "You see Piper Kay today, you tell her I'm looking for her."

"Yes, sir, I will."

The door closed with a determined bang.

WHAT THE HELL WAS PIPER thinking? Walker rubbed Josie's back as they walked. She'd forced them together because she said they were both stubborn, but dammit to hell, she had no right to put Josie in such a bind. He'd wanted her to take the job for a long time, but to trick her into moving, that was unbelievable even for Piper. He opened the door to the café and found a table in the back. He ordered two rancher specials, and coffee before he'd even pulled back Josie's seat.

"Walker, I really had no idea."

"Oh, I know, baby." He reached his hand out to cover hers on the table. "How did she get you to sign the contracts and not know who you were working for?"

Josie shrugged. "I don't know, we were talking, and she slid the forms under my hand, referred to you as Walt, gave me a pen, and as we talked, I signed. Your signature wasn't on it, so we don't have to go through with it."

"Oh, Piper took care of that for me. What a considerate sneak." Coffee came. Both took a sip of the hot brew.

"This is good," said Josie.

"Best coffee for miles around. You know, I wanted you to have that job."

"I didn't know before Piper told me. Then Camille told me, and they kept telling me. I can't believe you held the position in hopes that I would take it. Why didn't you say something?"

"I was waiting for the right opportunity. You loved where you were at the time. I didn't want to take you away from something you enjoyed *and,*" he added, exaggerating the conjunction, "I had hoped we would grow closer, stronger together, then I'd ask you."

They both took another quiet sip. "I missed you yesterday." Josie didn't look at him when she spoke.

Walker shook his head at the irony. "The only time you gracefully accepted help."

"Touché. I didn't have a choice. I needed the job, so I had to move fast. I couldn't do it alone and meet the deadline."

"Another Piper special. Well, the Knights got you into this mess, and we'll get you out."

"No, it's okay, I ..."

"Josie, we aren't discussing this until we get some food inside. Here come our plates, and I'll get us more coffee. We are going to enjoy the food and then figure this out. Deal?"

She smiled. "Deal."

Walker was relieved Josie decided to give in. If putting her up against a wall forced her to ask, or at least accept help, he wasn't above pushing a little. And being with her felt so right, he knew she was the one, so no matter how hard they had to work for this relationship to succeed, he was up for it. Josie was worth the effort. He took a bite of breakfast and moaned his pleasure.

"I'm hungry, and this is so good." He made another groan of satisfaction.

"I remember that sound," came a quiet voice from across the table.

Walker choked and grabbed his water. After clearing his throat, he spoke. "Sugar, you shouldn't say things like that when a man is off his guard. I could have choked to death."

He watched Josie take a sip of coffee and lean back. "Sorry."

She said it in a "sorry-not-sorry" way. He wanted to kiss her, spank her, and then bed her, in that order, but he wouldn't. Well, not this morning anyway.

Walker swallowed and took another sip of coffee before leaning back in his chair. "Any idea what we're going to do about this little mess?"

Josie put her fork down and gave Walker her serious expression. He knew that determined look and waited for her to respond, hoping he agreed with what she said. "I really don't know. I'd like to say that I could just go back to Austin and put Piper on the persona non grata list until she has groveled sufficiently, but that won't work for either of us."

Walker stared at Josie for a minute. "Would you consider taking the job? I really do need an assistant, and I've been holding out for too long. You know a lot about the job already, and I can teach you the rest."

"Can we work together?" Josie was biting her lip, a tell Walker knew well. She was contemplating saying yes. His heart and cock jumped.

"I think so. But are you asking if we will fight? Probably. Will we have some growing pains? Yep. Am I damn glad you're here? Oh, hell, yes. What do you say? Can we give this a go?"

"Just the job or us?"

"Good question. I'd like to say both. What do you think about that scenario?"

"I'm still not going to ask for help."

"And I'm still not going to be okay with that, but I have a proposition. Let me help you learn that sometimes, asking for help is not only better but advisable. I propose that when you can handle it, then go for it. But if you have something that might put you or others in danger without help, you ask for it. Big or small. If you don't, I can offer my own incentive to help you remember to ask the next time."

"I'm not sure I like that."

"Try it?" Walker gave his irresistible encouraging smile. Josie had told him before that when he gave her the "pleading" look. She was doomed. That was his plan.

"What kind of incentive?" Ah, there was her suspicious nature.

"All kinds, but I get to give you consequences if you risk safety or health. I can give early incentives to ensure you don't forget if you like."

"I'm not so sure about this, but I do want to stop feeling so horrible if I ask for something little. Okay, but I can call a halt if I don't like it."

"How about a compromise? One month. If you've given it a month and want to stop, we will. Deal?"

She bit gently on her lower lip before soothing it with her tongue, a gesture so captivating that it nearly distracted Walker for the rest of the day.

"Deal, on one condition. You promise not to step in and do things for me unless it could be harmful or I have asked."

"I can handle that. But us being a couple, a real, full-time couple, has nothing to do with whether the incentives and consequences work. We continue to work on us as a team in all areas of life, regardless of the outcome of this little experiment. Right?"

She nodded. "I'd like that. I have to clean my apartment and go back to set up the duplex."

"If we are a couple again, we live together, like the last time you were on the ranch. Or," Walker put his hand up when Josie would protest, "you can put your things in the cabin I had cleaned out for my assistant, but you sleep with me, either in the cabin or the main house. Are we clear on that?"

Josie shivered and nodded. Walker smiled. "Eat up. We have a full day ahead of us, and it's almost ten."

Walker could tell Josie remembered how he liked to be in control. In the bedroom, she loved it. He would have to try hard not to carry their personal dynamic into the office. He had an uneasy feeling that this was his last chance to make Josie see they were meant to be together. He would have to curtail his more robust attributes until she was settled. Walker had to be a good boss and an even better boyfriend. Josie deserved it, and they deserved forever.

He had always thought he was good with women, but Josie forced him to up his game. She was worth the work. In the meantime, Josie would have to learn to lean on him when it was necessary. He intended to show her he would be there for her when she needed him. And that she needed him as her Daddy. It was a part of who they were that worked but she preferred it behind closed doors. He didn't care where it was but understood that was a firm line for her. He would make it move to their private times to include the bedroom.

His goal was to keep Josie for his own and to help her see that asking was not weak or a show of incompetence. But first things first, he'd help to get her settled. Walker hadn't been this excited and anxious since he had asked the prettiest girl in his class to go to the dance in middle school. His whole future was riding on this working out well.

Chapter 5

The day had been long but rewarding. At first, Josie had been resistant to Walker's organizing the move of her things again, this time from the duplex to the ranch, but with only a few words, he had the place emptied and re-installed in the cabin, even her bed re-assembled, by dinner. She grudgingly appreciated that she didn't have to worry about it. Josie also allowed Walker to drive her in his truck back to Austin to retrieve the rest of her things. Finally, he'd called the cleaning service associated with the apartments and set up an appointment for them to clean the place.

"Perfect. The manager will have the key." Josie watched him end the call before she spoke.

"You shouldn't have done that. I can clean my apartment."

"Yes, but do you want to? Do you have the time? Energy?"

"Walker, we can't all do what we want. Well, most of us can't. Sometimes you do things because you have no choice, and I didn't want to spend $200 on someone else cleaning up."

"You didn't, I did or rather the ranch did, and it was money well spent."

"I'll pay you back."

"If you even try, I'll roast your rear. I did it because I know what you would have done. You would have worked all week learning a new job, then rushed here on Friday night, even though you were exhausted. You'd have cleaned as much as you could and slept on the floor. The next morning, you would have worked like a dog to get everything done, then finishing late, you'd have driven back to the ranch, beat, and dangerous behind the wheel."

"But I wouldn't have spent 200 dollars."

"No, but you would have put your safety at risk by driving both ways exhausted, and your health at risk by not getting enough rest before you started the next week. Not on my watch. We've discussed this often enough. You know safety and health are my absolutes."

"Fine, I'll give in on this, but I'm not a child. I can do more, handle more, and survive more than you obviously realize. We have to find a middle ground."

Josie watched as his eyes darkened, and thunder rumbled in his voice. He brought her closer, his words intimate and low. "You know I'm right." She shivered.

"We have to both compromise," she whispered. "It won't work if it's just me."

The gentleness that replaced the storm was disconcerting. His lips came closer still, touching hers with tenderness. He whispered back. "Agreed. Thank you for giving in this time."

"I won't always," she said.

Walker kissed her. "Understood." He kissed her again.

"Hardly ever." She breathed. He kissed her cheek.

"Mmm, hmm." He moved his lips to her eyes.

She groaned. "Walker, we need to get going. It's late."

His forehead met hers lightly. "I want you so badly."

"I know. The need is mutual, but we have to go home."

Walker grinned. "Home. I like hearing you say that about the ranch. I'd like it more if you were spread-eagled, naked, in the middle of my bed waiting for me when you said it." Josie quivered. Walker smiled. "My baby wants that too."

One more slow, sweet kiss items and stepped back briskly, snagged her backpack, the bag with the final retrieved household items, and moved Josie toward the door.

Walker insisted that he search the building for the manager that wasn't in his office. Mrs. Manager said he was in the building somewhere and said she didn't handle any of the property issues.

Josie nodded. "I'll give it to him later."

"We aren't coming back to give him the key, Josie."

"Alright, but I know the building, so I can find him faster. I'll meet you outside."

"It's too late for you to be wandering the building unprotected."

"So, come with me."

"Is it that important to you?"

She deflated a little. "No."

"Then let me do this."

She yawned. "Okay."

Putting her in the car and connecting her seat belt, Walker kissed her lips, his tongue tracing the swollen red tissue before handing her the truck keys and shutting the door.

"Lock it and hold the keys. Hit the panic button if you need help," he said and then proceeded to wait until she had done so.

Exhausted, Josie took a few moments to reflect on the insanity her life had plunged into since saying yes to Piper. That woman was a force unto herself, and as much as Josie understood that she only wanted what was best for herself and Walker, it was the wrong way to go about it. Piper hadn't taken their feelings into consideration. What if it had been too awkward? Or if Walker, being the same type of man that Piper herself was married to, had not allowed the manipulation out of principle and had refused to make a go of this?

Piper hadn't considered Josie either. She had broken it off with Walker the first time because the environment had gotten too intense. The second time, they knew each other, so they weren't in the learning stage. They had tried to fit together without change. Both had passively refused to accept the challenges that lay before them.

It had been a kind of attempt to be together without rocking the boat, but it hadn't worked because neither of them could accept the other person not changing. Walker had decided Josie needed to be ready to let him in on a deeper level, so he had stepped away from them. She'd let him go because he was right, and she didn't see a way around who she was. That was two months ago. She had been miserable, and evidently, so had Walker. He was bossy, and she was stubborn. How were they going to make this work?

Life had thrown them together to make another go. The third time was a charm, right? This time Walker was different. Josie hoped she was different too. This go-round, adjustments were expected and inevitable. No walking on eggshells. Josie would try to allow others to lend a hand when she needed it, and Walker would have to tone down his need to rule every situation. Could they do it? Who knew, but she was determined to try because she did have feelings for Walker, ardent, knee-weakening, core quivering feelings that she wanted to explore further. Time to be an adult and conquer her fears.

Piper and Jackson Knight, both forces to be reckoned with when they were on a mission, were the people to call if you had to get something done. Josie was just the slightest bit intimidated by them when they were in "takeover" mode. She wondered how their little daughter would turn out. Janine was mellow so far. Wouldn't that be a laugh if the most kick-butt couple she knew had a laid-back daughter?

Camille and Sawyer Knight were the cutest couple. They had three small children, and while Sawyer was the youngest Knight brother, he was no longer the kiss 'em, bed 'em, leave 'em guy he had been when Josie first met him several years ago. Camille was his first and only love. After an incident that took Camille away for a few years, she was back, married to Sawyer, and working part-time as the school nurse. Camille was upbeat, intelligent, and the most nurturing person Josie had ever met. And she loved babies no matter the species. Colton, their youngest, was in danger of being cuddled so much that Sawyer said if she didn't put the boy down, he'd never crawl. He wasn't wrong.

Walker knocked on the driver's side window, and Josie opened the door, handing him the keys. In a few seconds, the Bluetooth took up the call he was on, and Walker pulled out of the parking lot.

"Jackson, it doesn't matter that she meant well, you and I both know she stepped over the line. Hell, the line is so far behind her, she'd need binoculars to find it again."

Josie listened to the brothers' conversation over the speaker system. "Yeah, I get it," said Jackson with a resigned sigh. "How's Josie? I bet she was fit to be tied."

"She was a little shocked that Piper would do that. I mean, she thought they were friends."

"Do I need to try to smooth things over with her?"

Walker looked over at Josie, motioning for her to speak. She shook her head. It seemed Walker didn't understand why she kept quiet. He didn't seem to get that she was embarrassed that she had been so easily duped. She also remembered that awkward moment in time when she and Walker had realized what Piper had done.

"I'll take care of that, but really, you better have a come to Jesus moment with your girl. When I see her, I'll let her know that anything like that ever happens again, she risks our relationship."

"Well, you can't excommunicate her."

"No, but I can simply stay away from her as much as possible. I love the girl, always have, but you have to know, this is the last time she gets into Josie's or my business."

"Understood. Hey, so now what are you going to do about needing an assistant? You know that Carrigan girl might have skills."

"I've got it covered."

Jackson hesitated. "Alright. Well, do we need to help Josie with rent or whatever? I mean, we can't leave her holding the bag for this move and whatnot."

"Nope, got that sorted out too."

He reached his hand over the center console and squeezed Josie's thigh lightly before settling his hand next to, but not touching, her mound. She wiggled away, slightly, and he tapped her firmly, giving her a half head shake to stop her from removing him from his spot as he continued his conversation.

"Really." Jackson's voice sounded a bit suspicious. "She already moved out of the duplex?"

"Yep."

"Uh-huh. Did she have a place to go?"

"She found a place."

"Right. And is Belinda setting the table for one more?"

"Might be."

"That's what I thought. Well, good for you, man. Josie is a great gal, and I know, if you both worked at it, you'll both see that this is who you should be with."

"I'm thinking that. Hey, gotta go, but do me one favor besides giving that woman of yours a few swats for me. Don't tell her we worked it out. I want her to sweat a little."

Jackson chuckled. "No problem."

Walker disconnected. Josie hesitated to ask, but she needed to know. "Walker?"

"Yes." He must have heard her voice waver because he shot her a quick, curious look before returning his attention to the road.

"Is Jackson going to, I mean, will he... what's he going to do?

"What do you think he's going to do?"

Josie shrugged, but she had a good idea. Jackson was a Knight, after all, but just saying the word embarrassed her.

"I think you know, but you're having a hard time saying it, so I'll help you, but sweetheart, you're gonna have to get over that at some point. I imagine they are going to discuss the events of the last few days. Jackson will be pacing and then sitting, but there's a hundred percent chance Piper will be discussing it from a prone position."

Josie could feel her face and neck grow hot. "Yeah, that's what I thought."

"You want to talk about it?"

"No." Josie wanted to talk about anything else, really.

"Okay, we'll shelve that conversation except, you know I spank. That hasn't changed. And you know I only do it when you agree. There are plenty of ways to work on bad habits, and it isn't the only foreplay out there. We have a growing repertoire."

Josie took a deep breath. "I thought we weren't going to talk about it."

"We aren't. I just needed to remind you that I do spank for pleasure and discipline, and while we haven't had much of either lately, we will. There will come a day that you will be in the same position that Piper is probably in right now, getting your ass spanked for putting yourself in danger or refusing help and getting hurt in the process. Piper is getting her conversation for a whole other reason. Besides, she likes it, and Jackson loves it. Not too much of a real punishment for her."

She couldn't respond. It was so hot, her face was melting off. Her belly was doing acrobatics. Her core was sizzling and damn if she didn't feel slippery. Right at that moment, Walker moved his hand to cup her mound and then gave it two little pats. With her center on high alert, she jumped with the added stimulation. She wasn't sure in the dark cab, but Walker looked like he was smiling. Rat.

As they pulled out onto the main road leaving Austin, Walker asked, "Why Tina?" And just like that, the subject changed.

"What? Tina? I don't..."

"Yes, where did Piper get the name Tina?"

"Oh. I don't know... oh, yes, I do. She said the assistant's name was Tina Gold, right?"

"Yeah."

"My full name is Josephine Christina Silver Rodriguez. Chris-Tina Silver-Gold."

"That little sneak. And you didn't catch it?"

"Crazy, I know, but I hardly ever use my middle name, and Silver is only on my birth certificate. The name isn't a last name or hyphen, so," she shrugged, "I never think of it. And I would not have tried to create a puzzle from Silver to Gold."

"Who does that?" Walker sounded amazed.

"Piper, evidently. She's inventive. I have to hand it to her."

"Good at getting her butt in a sling and earning a good tanning. She has always given Jackson a run for his money."

"But she kind of grows on ya, you know?"

"I know exactly. I sometimes think Piper pushes the envelope when she wants Jackson to address it. He, like Sawyer and I, is about consent, and I think when Piper begs, that's consent. Why don't you try to get a little sleep? We have about forty-five minutes until we're back at the ranch, and you can get a little rest."

"I won't wake up easily when we stop. I'll just stay awake."

"Baby, we have an early morning, and you've had a wild few days. Sleep. I'll take care of getting you into bed."

"I'll get myself into bed, thank you very much."

Walker paused, and Josie already regretted her words. "I'm sorry, Walker. My nemesis is rearing her head. I know you're just trying to take care of me. I'll try to sleep if you don't get irritated if I can't."

"Good. Go ahead and try."

WALKER PULLED INTO the ranch's long drive and was glad he was home. It had been a long, draining day, but they were done. The days when he had to drive to Austin to see his girl were over. Even though he hadn't gone to see her for a few months, he wondered if he would have been able to stay away. His feelings were so strong that he doubted it. When he had woken up this morning, nearly eighteen hours ago, he had no idea his life would do a complete 180, but here he was. Josie snored softly next to him, making his heart swell, and he was about to take her into bed. His bed. With him beside her. Yeah, he was damn tired, but he wouldn't change the outcome of today for anything.

The porch light was on, but he doubted anyone would be up. They all got up early and went to bed as soon as they were tired, so he was surprised when Sawyer met him at the door.

"Hey," Sawyer said. His curiosity was visible even in the shadows, but Sawyer would wait for Walker to speak.

"Hey. Can we talk in the morning?"

Without question, Sawyer nodded. "Yeah. I'll lock up. Need anything from your truck tonight?"

"Nah. Night."

"Night."

Walker had taken the downstairs suite his father had before he died to give Sawyer and Camille more room and privacy on the second floor. Belinda, their housekeeper, had a bedroom off the kitchen. Tonight, he was glad he didn't need to carry his girl up that long flight of stairs. She wasn't heavy, typically, but Walker was bone tired. He got the door open with a little fiddling and laid Josie on the bed. After a quick shower, he made sure the door was locked just in case his oldest nephew decided to come barreling into the room as he'd done enough times before to make it likely.

Then he stripped his girl down to her panties and bra. He thought about taking at least the bra off, but they hadn't been together in a few months. He didn't want her to believe he was taking what she wasn't offering. Walker stood back and remembered she hated to sleep in her bra, so he took that off, too. Panties stayed.

"Walker?"

"Hush, Sugar. You're in bed."

"Mmm-kay. Can I have a t-shirt?"

"Yes, baby."

"Thanks," she said as she rolled over and cuddled in.

She was perfect with her round bottom and perky breasts that were peaked from the cool air. They were more than a handful, but not a lot more making them perfect for him. He loved her so much. Now if he could only convince her of that. He pulled a clean tee out of his drawer and slipped it over her head. He knew she was a hard sleeper, but Josie had to have been bone-tired not to do more than curl up in a ball. He pulled back the covers from under her and laid them on top before stepping back.

She was the most beautiful woman he'd ever seen. Maybe others wouldn't think that, but he did. Her lips were pink and a little pouty as she slept. Her dark, chestnut hair was thick and shiny, not like his unremarkable dark brown, usually dirty by the end of the day, hair. Her nails were trimmed short with lavender polish to match her shirt today. Her long lashes covered her brown eyes of nearly the same chestnut, but with a glow of excitement and sometimes mischievousness behind them.

Josie was the first to volunteer help in any situation, but because of her mother's choice of lifestyle, she had suffered the results of her parent asking for too many handouts. It had caused Josie to refuse most help, whether she needed it or not. He'd work on it with her. Walker hoped that being around his family again, 24/7, would show her that it wasn't weak or taking advantage of others' generosity if she took some help now and again. He and his brothers helped each other without thinking. The only way they could keep the ranches going is if they worked together collaboratively. She would see that.

And if she didn't, he had his methods of making her see the error of her ways. But for now, he was too tired to think. He'd taken this week at a lesser pace because of his new assistant. Tomorrow that would translate to sleeping in an extra hour or two. If he could.

IT HAD BEEN THREE DAYS since Josie had slept in Walker's bed. She'd asked for time to organize the cabin and he had agreed but now he was getting irritable, and so was she. After three heated arguments about nothing important, and a door slamming event that ended up with her sitting gingerly in her office chair, Josie figured they had finally gotten the rubble out of the way, and they could settle down.

"Your place set up yet?" asked Walker as he tossed his work hat on the desk. He'd been out checking on the new livestock.

"Yes."

"Good, we can sleep there tonight."

"What?"

Walker sat on the edge of his desk that faced the side of her workspace. He liked his desk away from the wall; she preferred hers against. So, she'd moved her heavy furniture around so that it faced the wall, and she only had to turn her head to see who was coming in the door. Walker tried to get her to change her mind and turn it back to face his desk, but she couldn't work that way.

"Too many distractions."

After a few minutes of trying to change her mind, he gave up and focused on the fact that she had moved the desk herself.

"It must have been heavy to get it against the wall."

"Not really. I mean, it's heavy, yes, but I didn't need to lift it, just push it."

Walker looked at her for another moment, and it appeared as though he was going to say something but evidently decided not to because he reiterated what he'd said when he walked in.

"We are sleeping in your bed tonight. Unless you want to sleep in mine. I'm not picky. Just know we are sleeping together tonight."

Josie twirled in her seat to stare at him, face to face. She crossed her arms and gave him her, "you've got to be kidding" look. He didn't appear impressed.

"I gave you some time to settle in and get your things set up, but now we are sharing a bed. And we will be doing so from here on out. Don't act so surprised. We have slept together most nights we could since we first were together. I intend to continue the tradition."

"But I don't really have dinner food yet."

"We can eat at the house."

"Things are put away, but it's not cleaned up, really."

"Look, you choose where we sleep, but we sleep together. Now, what does our breeding stock inventory look like?"

Josie wasn't ready to explain that she was afraid that if they were intimate, then she would lose the respect of the ranch hands. Several of them already treated her like a candy shop treat: sugary sweet and enticing them to take a bite. She hadn't mentioned it to anyone because she knew the others needed to get used to the fact that Josie was there to stay and that she knew her stuff. She tried not to monopolize Walker's time, but they still spent a lot of the workday together.

She was learning the ropes. Wasn't that normal? What she didn't know on the ranch, she had Walker to teach her. She hoped the obvious brushing up against her backside when Walker wasn't around or accepting something from her hand and holding on for longer than required, touching their fingers to hers, would soon end.

One cowboy, in particular, was too familiar far more than once. Yesterday morning, while she was about to throw a saddle on Crescent, the gelding she liked to ride, Corey came up behind her. With his front to her back, he grabbed the leather from her hands and stepped around her just long enough to toss it on the horse. He stepped behind her again.

"I can do that. Thank you. I don't need your help."

"Maybe not, but you like it."

"You're Corey, right?" He nodded. "Well, for your information, Corey, I don't need or want your help."

She stepped out of his grasp that he had managed to gain again. She yanked the saddle off the horse's back and shoved it at the cowhand, not caring if he grabbed it or not. She stormed out of the barn with his jeering laughter following her. She didn't need any trouble, nor did she want the cowboys to think she couldn't handle things herself. They likely expected her to go running to the boss.

Today, she'd just shoved herself from the corner where one cowboy about her age had pinned her. He wasn't really trying anything, just intimidating her.

"I know Walker thinks he did the right thing bringing in a woman to help him run the day-to-day operations, but he should have picked someone different, a man who knew the job or at least a woman tough enough to handle things. You have soft hands, and while that might be great in bed, it is nothing that lasts long on a ranch. Why I bet, you ain't never even lived on a ranch before."

"You'd be wrong. I lived on this ranch and worked on the Clearwater. Now kindly move."

"I've found I kinda like this corner. I found some interesting goodies in it."

"I'll scream."

Feeling a bit panicked when he didn't get out of the way, Josie didn't know what to do. Walker was either at the Martin Place talking a deal or out with the hands working on something, but he was out of pocket for sure. He wouldn't be close enough to save her if it got worse. The cowboy smiled a nasty smile as though he knew her thoughts but said nothing more. Then an angry male voice boomed in the quiet, causing her to jump and the other man to twirl around quickly. Sawyer.

"The lady asked you to move. Now I'm an impatient man, so maybe she was giving you more time to comply than I think necessary, but when a woman asks you to move out of her way, you move. If I ever see this again, or behavior similar, you'll pack your sack."

"Now, I wasn't causing her no harm."

"Renfro, you were intimidating her or trying to, and that's more than enough to give you the boot. I don't guarantee what Walker will do when he finds out. Now get out of my sight before I change my mind."

Renfro hesitated as if he were going to say something but decided against it. The sound of his boots treading heavy and angry over the wooden floor gave her a sense of foreboding. A tremor of adrenaline drop raced through her muscles.

"You good, sweetheart?"

"Hmm? Oh, yeah, I'm fine. Thanks for stepping in, but I could have dealt with it. I've handled him before."

"Excuse me? What did Walker say?"

"Nothing."

"Nothing? I can't see that man saying nothing when his woman is being harassed by one of the ranch employees on Knight land."

"Well, I... um... didn't tell him exactly."

"No? Well, do you mind telling me what you did tell him, exactly?"

Sawyer's tone had changed, and she felt just the tiniest bit chastised. Her shoulders drooped a little. "I didn't tell him at all."

Sawyer watched her a minute. "Why not?"

"Because I didn't want there to be any disruption because I'm here. Some of the guys already think I'm incompetent. One even called me a freeloader out for Knight money. I didn't want to have another reason for them not to like me."

Sawyer whistled. "Honey, better they get their ass chewed than you."

"Why is it either/or situation?"

"Well, the way I see it is you and Walker are a team, and teams keep each other apprised of situations. That way things don't get out of hand. It's kind of like this. You're watching your friend's dog. You're doing a good job, but the day before the owner comes to pick him up, a stray comes out of nowhere and jumps the dog. You're able to get him away, and the harm is minimal. A little scrape, one tooth mark, but it's stopped bleeding, so you clean it and go on. The owner comes and picks up their dog. Some weeks later, you run into that friend and ask after the dog. Your friend says he died. Somehow, he got rabies even though he was vaccinated. They were unable to save him because the owner didn't take him to the vet in time.

"Now, it's not your fault the dog contracted rabies, but you worry that if you had told the owner about the fight, she would have been alerted and at the first sign of change, would have gotten him in and likely saved her pet."

"You're saying that if I don't tell Walker about these things, he won't know the danger is out there and if something really happened, he'd blame himself even though it wasn't his fault."

"That's the lesson."

"You're a little long-winded."

Sawyer chuckled. "I can be. I've got little inquisitive minds following me around. Now, Josie, I'm not telling Walker, but I'm going to assume you are. I'm not going to watch what I say in order to keep this a secret. Your best bet is to tell him what happened today and mention any other issues you've had. Tell him about your concern that it could make things worse if he overreacts because he is going to want to do just that."

"Can I think about it?"

Sawyer checked the wall clock. "I wouldn't wait too long. Dinner is in three hours." He dropped a kiss on Josie's cheek. "And Josie? You belong to this family now, and we take care of our own, whether it means knocking a misdirected ranch hand down a notch or setting our family member straight. Don't forget it is better if Walker doesn't find out the way I did. Much better." Sawyer strolled out of the barn.

Josie followed as her stomach tightened in anticipation of making Walker truly angry with her or his employees. She had never seen him more than upset. Even with Piper, he stayed fairly level, given the circumstances. Would he keep it together in this one, too?

Taking a deep breath, Josie went back to the office. She breathed a sigh of relief when Walker wasn't there, then she started worrying he wouldn't make it back in time for her to tell him what happened. Josie envisioned Sawyer spilling the beans, and Walker would be fit to be tied. She wouldn't get out of that situation without some repercussions.

Finally, after worrying about the fallout for almost half an hour, Josie was able to dive deep into her data entry. The ranch hadn't done much in the way of digital records other than what was necessary. Part of her job was to change all that.

Josie was making headway when she heard familiar boots on the stairs. The office was situated above the inventory barn that serviced the house cook and the ranch hand's cook. It also had a variety of extra supplies in general for the ranch. Her body fairly vibrated with anticipation, both good and bad. Josie was always glad to see her man, but today, she was dreading it as well. What if he blamed her for the incidents? Maybe he would think she was inviting the behavior. She wanted to throw up.

Walker tossed his hat on his desk and walked over to give her a sensual, sexy kiss that had her melting in her chair. He stared at her a second before taking a step back.

"What's wrong?"

"Why do you ask?"

"Because you look like a girl who hopes her boyfriend can slip out before he gets caught by her daddy. Come clean. You'll feel better."

"Better take a seat Walker, I think we have a little problem."

Chapter 6

The first thing that ran through his brain was that he had pushed the sleeping arrangements too hard, and now she wanted out.

"Listen, baby, if you don't want to share a bed yet, I can wait."

Josie looked confused, which baffled him. Hell, she wasn't going to say that, and now he'd watered that seed of thought. "So, not that, I take it."

"No, not that. I'm good with sharing your bed. I'm not good with being harassed."

He was on his feet before he could think. "Come again? Who the hell is harassing you?"

Her hands came out as a barrier to his outrage. "It's not as bad as it sounds, Walker, really. Don't get upset."

"Honey, how can I not get upset. Who is harassing you? What happened? If I employ him or her, they are gone."

"I used the wrong word. Harass was too strong. More like disrespectful, kind of bothering me."

"Josie, I know you well enough that you take any problem as a challenge to overcome. So, if it was enough for you to say something, then you didn't over-dramatize the issue. Now tell me who is causing you trouble."

He needed to settle down, or he would scare her into not sharing. He went back to sit on the corner of his desk and forcibly stopped clenching his hands. Walker took a deep breath, quieted his tone and gentled his delivery.

"Well, I'm trying not to do it all myself, like you wanted me to do. While I could have continued to handle it, I've decided to let you help."

"And I'm happy you're trying to follow our agreement, but baby, I still need to know who it is and what he or she did."

"Nothing, really."

"Josie don't ruin this by being evasive now. What happened?"

"Okay. Corey violated my personal space yesterday again. He was inappropriate with his body in proximity to mine and said I wanted it when I tried to stop him. Not a big deal, but I felt uncomfortable."

"Again? What the hell? You've only been here a week. I'm going to break his immature neck."

"No, this is why I wasn't ever going to tell you, Walker. I dealt with it myself because I could, but I didn't want to make you angry like you are. The ranch hands are going to resent me if I tattle on every little thing. If you have to talk to Corey, and I understand you believe you do, just do it privately. And for heaven's sake, don't fire him."

Walker paused before speaking, knowing he had to slow his roll. He tried to sound as reasonable as he could regardless of how he really felt, which was to wring Corey's scrawny neck.

"What I'm curious about is it sounds as though this isn't the first time you've had trouble, so what made you tell me now?"

Josie looked at her tightly folded hands. "Partly, it's what I said, I want to try to be better about accepting help but more than that, I was afraid you would find out if I continued dealing with him on my own."

Walker crossed the space between his desk and hers and came around to where Josie was sitting. "I'm sorry this happened to you. I employ good workers that are good men. Corey is young, and because of that, I'll let him keep his job this once. If it happens again, after I have a talk with him, he packs his sack. You got me?"

"I do. Thank you for not going overboard."

"Now, you have a little educating due you as well. You should have told me the first time Corey was inappropriate. Three swats for hanging on to the information after the first time."

"Walker, it only happened twice. I handled it the first time and told you the second time."

"So, the second time was today."

"Yesterday. But to be fair, I didn't see you except at dinner yesterday, and you were late. I went home because I was tired, remember?"

"I do, but you could have told me this morning."

"Right, but I didn't think it would happen again."

"Next incident that should be dealt with by the owner, you will tell me right away. Not ask for help, simply inform me of who I need to set straight. This is a safety issue. He could have thought since nothing was said the first time, that you might even have welcomed it."

"Yeah, pretty sure that wasn't what he was thinking after either time."

"Lean over the desk, baby."

"Walker. I said I didn't know, and when it happened again, when I knew he wouldn't take no for an answer, I came to you. You don't want me running to you every time something happens, only if it continues."

"Look, we need to go to supper, but you're getting three swats for a reminder. If you keep anything like this from me again, it will be much worse for you, hear me?"

Josie nodded.

"I need to hear a yes, sir."

Josie rolled her eyes and made a production of her irritation as she rose from her chair. "Yes, sir. I want to renegotiate."

Walker helped her over the desk. "I bet you do. Five swats."

"Hey, you said three."

"Yep, three for the slow disclosure and two for the attitude."

"You can't spank me for attitude. I'm an adult. And it isn't health or safety."

"Oh, sweetheart, with you, it will be the one thing I think I'll be swatting your ass for most often. Now, tell me you aren't okay with this setup, and we stop. But if I have to find another incentive, I think denied orgasms might be a good alternative."

"Walker, I better get some damn good sex out of this."

"Later, sweetheart. Lord woman, it's just a few swats, not an all-out spanking."

"I just hate knowing in advance."

"Noted."

Josie made some very unladylike notes of disagreement, but Walker waited for her to settle down and to make sure it's a bargain she was still willing to keep. She lay calm after a minute.

Without another word, Walker swung and slapped her butt hard. Not as hard as he could, by any means, he'd never do that, but hard enough that she jumped and whimpered. Then the little scamp wiggled her bottom. Moving target. The second and third were equally hard but no more than the first. The fourth and fifth were well-aimed just to hit the space where her butt and thighs met. The sweet spot. One below either cheek, her hissing told him it got through to her. Then he rubbed her backside soothingly and leaned down to nip at her fleshy cheeks. She squealed and then laughed.

"What are you doing?"

"Making it all better." Walker stood and gave her rear end a lighter pat. "Let's go have supper so you can take me to bed and ravage me."

"Ooh, I like that."

"Yeah, I thought you'd think that was exciting."

"You mean, I really can?"

"You can really dream about it. Now grab your things, and let's get out of here." Walker placed his arm around her waist and walked Josie to the main house, all the while thinking about how he was going to have his discussion with Corey without handing him his ass.

As they entered the house, supper was just starting.

"Hey, you didn't wait for me," said Walker in a joking manner.

"Sorry, Uncle Walker," said Lily, her mouth partially filled with corn, "but we were hungry."

"I'll forgive you, squirt." Lily grinned and shoveled in more food. "This time." He reached over and ruffled the five-year-old's hair.

Josie was deep in conversation with Camille when she heard Walker speak to Sawyer as he filled his plate. "Josie just told me she was, to use her words, 'disrespected' and 'her personal space violated' by one of the hands."

"I'm glad she told you. I caught Renfro penning her into the corner today, using intimidation tactics to try to scare her. She's one tough woman. I was going to fire him but thought I should give a warning first. I think Josie was afraid it would make things harder around here if she got someone fired right off even if it was his own fault, and not hers. I hope I set her straight." Sawyer leveled a questioning look at Josie before taking another bite of dinner.

"Renfro? Don't you mean Corey?"

"Corey? No, it was Renfro, and he's old enough to know better."

"Yes, he is, and I would have fired him," announced Walker.

"I told him I would if it happened again," confirmed Sawyer. "I'm glad Josie told you. I was worried she would have tried to sweep this behavior under the rug. It does no one any good to ignore things like that. He had her pinned in the corner, and when she asked him to leave, the sorry cuss refused."

Josie suddenly wasn't hungry any longer. "Tell Belinda I enjoyed her dinner. I've got things to finish tonight, so I'll see you all in the morning."

"Sit, sweetheart. You didn't eat much, why don't you try a little more?"

"I'm really full." She wanted to throw up.

"Still, I'd like you to wait until I'm done, and I'll go with you."

He spoke casually, but Josie could hear the undertones of confused irritation. She knew that it didn't bode well for her evening events. Her heart raced as her face heated.

"Okay. Let me just run to the ladies while you finish."

"Absolutely. While you are in there, try to remember why you only told me about Corey, not Renfro."

"Corey, too?" asked Sawyer.

"Yep. Evidently, two employees have issues that will be addressed first thing in the morning. Tonight, I have other fish to fry."

"Why are you gonna fry fish tonight, Uncle Walker? We have dinner already," asked Lily.

"Don't you know anything, Lily? He means he has other things to do." Eli shook his head in exasperation. "Girls."

Camille spoke sharply. "Elijah Knight, that was rude and unnecessary. Apologize to Lily and the rest of us at the table."

"But mom..."

Sawyer cleared his throat, giving all the incentive his son needed to offer his apology to his sister.

"Thank you, Eli. After dinner, you'll clear the table."

"Aww, dad."

"Sawyer," started Camille. Her word was met with a raised eyebrow of warning.

"Cami, we can talk about it after dinner."

No arguing in front of the children was a big rule the couple had. Josie had thought it was a dumb rule because people fight, but after seeing the united front they gave and the way the children minded so well, she understood. Camille had once told her that Sawyer always made it sound like he made all the rules, and while he was often the enforcer, it was Camille that made many of the rules. However, she tended to be more arbitrary about enforcement. That was why Sawyer appeared so inflexible. It was a good team. Josie wanted that.

Josie slipped out of her chair during the little exchange, hoping to get some distance between her and Walker until she had a chance to figure out how to explain that she told about one person and not another. The reason was Renfro worried her, Corey didn't. How was she going to explain that she hadn't mentioned Renfro because she thought he might do something worse than pin her against the wall? He didn't want her here. Corey was just immature.

She flipped the light and fan on in the bathroom, hoping it would give her time to slip away. She took off out the back door and raced to hide behind the closest barn. She stayed there for a little bit, sitting on the new grass and wondering what she was doing. She'd left her backpack with her keys in it at the kitchen door. She also had taken off from Walker. This little escapade wouldn't end well; she just knew it.

She wasn't a child to run and hide, but right now, she felt exactly like a child who had already been spanked for being naughty and was making one bad choice after another. Funny, the men spanked their women, but they never laid a hand to their children. It was against their beliefs about raising children. She laughed. Only the Knight women got their fannies swatted.

She liked sexy swats, she loved the take-charge man Walker was, and she absolutely adored his loving, generous side. The discipline side of Walker was pretty new to her. She didn't hate it, and he never violated her right to say "no," when she actually meant it. He would not leave her for another because she didn't agree to the whole spanking thing, but somehow, she never did refuse him. The complete package made her pelvic region come alive in ways no other man had even come close.

Whenever Josie was distressed, she spoke to herself, out loud. "What is the matter with you? You have a guy who cares about you, a job you really like doing, friends you can count on and yet, you try to sabotage everything by keeping secrets and telling half the story, so you don't upset the apple cart."

She started to throw loose stones at the ground in front of her. "Walker is probably so angry he won't want me here anymore. He'll think he can't trust me and maybe he's right. I can't trust myself not to take care of things alone."

But it was more than that. Josie wanted to be what Walker needed, what he thought she could be. It was evident she was not that woman now, but she hoped she could be. "Why can't I just let people help me deal with things? Why do I have to always hear you, mama, in my head asking for the very shirt off someone's back and never feel embarrassed or concerned?"

Her mother had felt bad when she first heard that Josie was being bothered at school over her mother's panhandler ways, but she'd only been able to kiss her daughter and tell her to hold her head up high. But how could she? "There's no honor in asking for others to sacrifice for you when you could do it yourself, and if you can't, then you just find another way to get what you need. Mama, why couldn't you have just gotten a job?"

Josie threw the final three stones within her reach and stood up with determination. She dusted off the seat of her jeans. "I wish that were all that Walker was going to do; just dust my seat instead of spanking it. I hate spankings without sexy time. I can't help that I feel shame over asking, but he isn't going to understand. How could he? He never had to go, hat in hand, to borrow milk from a neighbor for your little siblings when both of you knew it wasn't a 'borrow' in the truest sense because you weren't going to replace it." Josie squared her shoulders to her imaginary foe. "I'm not apologizing for where I came from, Walker Knight."

Josie rounded the barn with determination. She would go right back into that house, get her backpack and walk out without any explanation. She didn't owe anyone anything. She paid her debts, or she didn't incur them. The economy of life demanded she not ask for any understanding if she didn't have any to give in return. Reciprocity was a great thing for those who were able to indulge. For those who were not equipped to respond in kind, one did not make use of anyone, for fear the price was too high. Those people who were responsible. Those who weren't like her mother.

Josie took two resolute steps when a deep voice resonated next to her. "Looking for this?"

"Oh shit. You startled me, Walker. How long have you been here?"

He tipped his hat up higher on his head and took a step closer, offering her the backpack. "Long enough to know we have put off this conversation for entirely too long, little girl, and I'm not waiting any longer. And your language will be part of our discussion."

Walker held out his hand to her and waited until she sighed heavily and took it before he handed her the bag. "Walker, I..."

He placed his finger over her lips. "Shush, honey. Let's just walk to the cabin and think. Time enough to figure this out once we get there. Yeah?"

She nodded. "Yeah."

She breathed a melancholy sigh, and yet, she felt right. Walker was the man for her, and somehow she had to get him to understand that changing the self-sufficient part of her wasn't like turning off a switch. It was going to take hard work and determination. Hopefully, it was a good thing, and he would see how hard it really was for her to push that thinking from the foreground. Josie knew she had to work out why she kept things to herself, why it was so hard to ask for help from him, and it seemed she already knew. Others, she understood, but why was it difficult to rely on Walker? If she didn't get a better handle on this, there would be no future for them, and that was something she couldn't contemplate.

They covered the distance to the cabin slowly, deliberately extending the time they were quietly holding onto each other. Josie was obviously thinking hard. Walker needed to process what he had overheard her saying. His girl had been blaming her mother's actions during Josie's formative years, for her own decisions today. Walker knew that it was time she took responsibility for her own actions, and in doing that, she would break free of the stigma of her childhood. First, he had to get her to see a few home truths.

Chapter 7

When they arrived at the cabin, he wondered how she had found the time to plant the flowers on the walk and the window boxes. Those window boxes had sat with dirt sans flowers forever. The spots of color brightened up the well-loved log cabin and gave it a homey feel he liked. His girl had so much talent and so many things going on with her that Walker wondered if he even knew her at all. Obviously, living in the city curbed some of her abilities. She didn't have one plant in her old apartment.

Josie was a force of nature on some days or with some issues, like the other day when he just wanted to put the inventory on paper, this first time, and then enter it in the computer later. Ignoring Walker's instructions, Josie showed up with her small backpack, something she usually wore, and instead of a notebook and writing utensil coming out of her bag, as he had requested, out came a book size front pack that held a tablet, stylus, and mini scanner.

"I said we take this headcount the hands-on way." He wasn't happy she had disregarded him.

"Look, I have five-plus years of filing left in that office. I also have logs to review, payroll to create, and that is just the beginning. If I can download immediately instead of re-entering, yay me."

Walker was irritated, but he could see her point. "Okay, techno girl, here is how we count..."

He had to hand it to her, Josie got the inventory done, downloaded it, and he had it in his email when they arrived back at the office. This rancher wasn't ready for the cloud yet. Josie said she would handle the security and backups. Good thing. Walker smiled at the memory because he'd still wanted to paddle her bottom for not following his instructions, but she had made a good point. She had agreed to an incentive over not asking for assistance when needed. Josie didn't need any in this particular scenario, so sadly, he had to put that idea to bed. She had won her argument and set the ground rule parameters.

He had also brought Josie to bed and teased and taunted her, spanking her for funishment. She'd come so hard he thought she'd hurt herself. He hadn't wanted to make more work, just teach her how to do it accurately the first time. Yes, his girl was smart, but sometimes she simply needed to listen to the boss, even if her way was more expedient.

Tonight, something was up. Walker knew why he was upset with her but not why she only told some of what had happened. He was glad he overheard a portion of her thoughts as she spoke aloud to herself, but not enough to know where to go from here, so a fishing trip was in order. Walker loved fishing, and this expedition would prove to yield much better results if he played his cards right. He followed her into the cabin that he saw she had locked. Except she left the windows open, causing a safety issue. Probably not much of one as the ranch was secure, but she was a woman alone at times. Yet, it showed her conflicting thoughts of being safe but not quite. He could start things there.

"Glad I don't have to tell you to lock the door, even on the ranch, except, it does no good if your windows are open, baby."

She shrugged. "No full-sized man could get in, and I don't worry about the women on the ranch."

She went into the kitchen to make tea. Walker followed her and leaned his hip on the counter in the corner of the room as he watched her turn the electric kettle on. "Why are you worried about the men on the ranch?"

"I didn't say that." Josie was avoiding his eyes.

"You did. You said you didn't worry about the women, and no full-sized man could get in the windows, both implying you are worried a man would."

"Well, I think it's just a good precaution."

"I agree, but why particularly are you concerned with men on the ranch? You were never worried before."

"I was naïve before, Walker." She yanked open the refrigerator and pulled out milk. "I thought people were generally good. I've learned that isn't true."

She pulled cookies out of the jar and poured two big mugs of hot water. She knew he liked herbal tea at night, so he didn't stay awake. She threw two Berry Medley Delight tea bags in Walker's cup with one-half teaspoon of sugar. She had decaf black tea and two teaspoons of sugar because she liked hers hot, strong and sweet, with a touch of milk. Walker grabbed the cups, and she brought in the cookies.

Once they were set up, Walker pulled her close to him on the sofa, putting his arm around her shoulders and then slid it down around her waist, tugging her even closer. Josie hesitated before leaning her head to rest on his chest.

"Why do you feel you can't trust men on the ranch now? Is it because of Renfro and Corey?"

Josie shrugged. Walker tapped her outer thigh just hard enough for Josie to understand the warning. "Maybe. I mean, I had no idea they thought they could touch me that way or say those things to me. I might have stood up for myself, but I'm not stupid. I can't trust they aren't going to continue or go to something worse. Better to be on your guard than to be taken unawares."

"Hell, baby, I'll protect you. I'll fire them."

"Oh, Walker, I love that you would say that, but you can't keep me safe all the time. You certainly can't fire every man that is disrespectful to me. It's a ranch with some rough around the edges men. They have to be to do the job. That isn't the problem. The trouble is that some of those same men have no personal boundaries."

Josie stopped to think, and Walker could see she was trying to word things right. "Josie, I will never allow someone to be inappropriate with you. There are other women, and now children, on the ranch. It simply can't happen.

"I know, but Camille and I are different because we are with Knight men. Camille is married, I'm not, so I could still be intimidated off the ranch. She doesn't need to work on the ranch, I do. I'll need to do things all over this place, and I can't worry about needing an escort, nor can I worry that they are timing their attacks based on whether you are around or not. The work you do will become twice as onerous because you're worried about me. No, I can handle things myself. Besides, I need to take care of it without you to show they can't push me around."

"I don't agree, but tell me why you think that?"

Josie turned, aiming her disbelief at him. "What do you mean, you don't agree? Your ranch hands think I'm after you for your part of the Knight assets. They think I'm incompetent because your assistant should have been a man, evidently or some crazy ass off the grid type of woman."

"Renfro?"

"Yes."

Walker kissed her temple and then her lips, taking possession with slow, sweet heat.

"Sweetheart, Renfro thinks he should be a manager, just like Cody, and when we refused to consider him, he said he should at least be my or Sawyer's second. We both declined the suggestion. He's a good worker but a hothead, and he makes rash decisions when he's irritated. Ranching requires clear thinking in all situations."

"Well, pinning me in the corner is a bad choice. I nearly cracked Renfro's nuts for him."

Walker burst out laughing, squeezing her in a tight hug. "I can see him going around with a metal athletic cup from now on."

Josie flashed him a smile before it quickly disappeared. "It's not really funny, Walker."

"No, I can see it isn't. Why didn't you tell me?"

She shrugged and leaned over to sip her tea. Still a little too hot but soothing. "Because the others would have figured I ran and told you so they could get in trouble. Like I ran to tattle to my daddy."

"As they should. This Daddy is flaming mad. Corey is young and stupid, but once you're over the twenty-five-year mark, you need to have your shit together. Renfro is about thirty, long past the stupid line. He is getting consequences, and I'll make it clear to him that it wasn't you who spilled the beans. The result of harassing another worker, especially my lady, will get him nothing but trouble."

"Thanks, but can't you just let it lie?"

"Nope. Honey, what kind of man would I be if I let another man insult, intimidate, or upset my woman and not do anything?"

"But he'll blame me."

Walker turned and manipulated her so he could see her eyes. "Look, if I don't say anything, he'll either think you didn't tell, so he is free to continue bothering you, or I didn't care, with the same result. No, you need to let me handle both men. Yeah?"

She nodded. "Yeah, okay."

"Good." He reached for his tea, taking a healthy gulp. Josie did the same, feeling the comforting warmth tea always gave her as it permeated her very soul. She loved coffee too, but tea in the evening relaxed her.

"Now, what about your punishment?"

"Mine?"

"Yep. You would have never told me if circumstances hadn't put you in a precarious position."

"But Walker, I told you why I didn't tell you."

"And why did you run away?"

She shrugged. "I needed to figure things out."

"It's obvious we need to discuss many more things, but I think this is enough for tonight." Josie relaxed her shoulders. "Now go take your shower and climb in bed. Naked."

"I could do that so long as it's funishment, and you're joining me."

"On the bed or in the shower?"

"Both?"

"Then hit it, girl. I'll let you in first, and I'll be there in a couple of minutes."

Josie started toward the bathroom turning in Walker's direction. "And the punishment?"

"Will happen, but you'll make it through well enough."

"What if I call you Daddy and beg?"

Walker laughed. "Whatever floats your boat, but it won't get you out of your comeuppance, and for the record, I'm not Sawyer. He's a sucker for the name Daddy."

She frowned. "Fine. Whatever. It was worth a shot."

Walker snagged her as she again started toward the bathroom. "It was and whether you call me Daddy or not, I am your Daddy and don't you forget it."

Wrapping his arm around her waist, he held her in a half-bent position tight to his hip and landed a flurry of stinging swats. Josie's squeal of surprised realization had just begun when Walker was done and had her standing upright again. Waiting until she was steady, he pointed to the bathroom.

"Now, let's try this again in a more respectful manner, shall we? I don't know why the attitude, but I'm not playing fortress to your battering ram."

"That was presumptuous, Walker."

Josie stopped to rub her insulted backside. He could see she was uncomfortable, but he also saw her eyes. They weren't flashing with irritation but a slightly dazed look. He had no doubt she was upset about him taking her to task intellectually, but she was also in need of his particular brand of love that she had not been able to find anywhere else. That little burst of surprised spanks fueled her desires. His little firecracker's fuse was lit, and she was sizzling for the grand finale.

Walker deepened his voice for further effect. "Hands off, sweetheart. You let that settle in, and maybe you'll remember next time you want to be mouthy with me and cop an attitude, that I don't allow disrespect in my relationship. Not for either of us. And since I plan on keeping you forever, it won't be allowed in your future, so best to learn that lesson now. The more times I have to address it, the harder you're going to find sitting. Understood?"

"Walker, I didn't agree to that. We are not working on respect. You know I respect you. We are working on me, allowing others to help and learning to ask for help when needed."

"Respectfully."

"Look, I'm not a teenager."

"Oh, I didn't miss that, baby. Even in my most distracted state, I have never missed that."

Josie picked up her pace as though she were worried Walker would follow with an encore. Walker smiled at her response, but then the reason why there was any behavior adjusting resurfaced. No, they hadn't discussed her insecurities with their relationship or her need to show that she was more than capable of handling things in a while. That thinking came from her childhood, a time that she had been hurt and embarrassed if her self-talk was any indication. Now was the time to bring that out in the open, dissect its responsibility in her unsafe decisions and then get rid of it.

Finally, Josie needed to stop blaming her mother's past behaviors on her own current choices. It was fine to know where the tendencies came from, it was important to understand how earlier life influenced present thinking, but at some point, Josie needed to accept that decisions became hers alone.

If they were hers, right or wrong, Josie then would have no other option but to take ownership of them. She'd have to stop shifting the liability of her mother's life away from herself but also accept that her mother wasn't making Josie's choices now. Walker had no doubt that once that was accomplished, it would be easier for his girl to accept help when important to do so. He'd learned that from his cousin's wife. Jocelyn lived in Montana with her husband, Liam, and their large clan of O'Connors. She was a smart woman and a good therapist.

Stripping as he stood outside the bathroom door, Walker smiled. He was unraveling the mysteries of his girl. Life could only get better. Kissing Josie always excited Walker, doing it in the shower after such a long dry spell nearly unmanned him.

"Can I wash you?" she whispered sweetly, her lips swollen from his kisses.

His irrepressible groan was spontaneous. "I'd love that, but when I say stop, you need to do it. Agreed?" His lips heated a trail along her jaw, his tongue tracing the flames his lips left behind. Josie whimpered. Walker grew more urgent in his lovemaking.

"Yes, agreed."

Her hands were suddenly soapy and massaging every bit of skin she could touch. His smattering of chest hair was tangled in bubbles as her fingers played as they sculpted the curls on his chest. She moved up and over his broad shoulders and down his deltoids, following his muscular arm until she reached his hand and then returning to descend down his chest again, further to his suggestive line of hair leading her down the sexy pathway to his happy place. His thatch of dark hair surrounding his cock was soaped, and his ability to control himself was almost gone. He clenched his teeth and his ass. The woman knew how to entice him regardless of her denials to the contrary.

Walker concentrated on remaining in control of his cock, but after several more strokes, he gave up. "Stop, baby. You feel too good. I won't last."

Josie immediately released his cock to Walker's relief and angst. She moved to his flexed ass. Walker relaxed his tight hold on his control to allow Josie to spend some time enjoying his body as he was enjoying hers. She moved back to his cock, and that was his limit.

"Stop now. I'm going to rinse off so we can finish this in bed."

She lightened her hold but didn't stop. The wet slap that resounded in the enclosed space was immediately followed by an outraged cry. She squeezed the base of the soapy cock, helping him keep control, whether she knew that fact or not. It would have helped more if it had been his hand and not hers. Any touch from his girl excited Walker. But the woman didn't let go. Another smack echoed in the room, only slightly muffled by the water and then totally obliterated by her accompanying cry.

Her breath came with a gasp. "I'm sorry, I'm sorry. No more spanking my wet ass. That shit hurts."

His hand slid up her neck and grasped her hair tightly, his breath hot in her ear. He kissed her cheek.

"Watch the language, woman. I'm going to spank you as many times as it takes for you to listen to me and mind. I told you, minding me mattered. Hands, on the wall." His voice was dark, but his tone was gentle.

"It stings, please; I'll listen. I was just playing." She wasn't at all worried. He heard the over the top acting in her voice. She was having fun. He would give her more.

His hand tugged her hair again, causing her to look up into his passion-filled eyes. "You were a naughty girl, teasing your man, and now I have to punish you. Get into the bedroom." His tongue licked the few droplets escaping her wet hair to travel down her cheek. He caught a few near her neck. His breath heated her cheek. "Wait for me on the bed, baby."

The worried look on her face was replaced by understanding. She knew he was going to play along. She was naughty in their sensual play; he would punish her the same way, and she would come. Her countenance was almost jubilant with the prospect of play, and her eyes were dilated with passion. He was feeling no less pull to satisfy his own sensual torment.

Whimpering and still rubbing parts of her on parts of him, she stepped out slowly from the shower. Bending to retrieve the towel that had fallen on the bathroom floor, her ass was displayed for him to touch, fondle, and spank as he saw fit. He slapped her pussy. Her grunt of surprise that quickly morphed to a moan told of her ache. She whined pleading for more, which earned her another bottom smack, sharper than the last. This time she left the bathroom, wiggling her bum in an enticing invitation. Walker grinned. She was such a minx. Time to do a little training on how to mind her man, sexy style. And set off the fireworks.

JOSIE WATCHED THE MAN of her dreams stride into the bedroom. The cabin was a good size and the bedroom bigger than one would expect, but when it housed Walker, the size diminished substantially. He was substantial. His chest was muscular, his arms and legs were bulky and hard covered in tanned, soft skin, warm and inviting. His expression was foreboding. Her belly and ass clenched.

In the shower, she'd been playing and got wrapped up in bringing him gratification. His deep murmurs of satisfaction, oohs, and aahs, proclaiming his enjoyment and the heated looks he'd given her, fueled Josie's desire to give him even more pleasure. She found it difficult to stop. If she hadn't had his cock lathered, she would have put her mouth on him and probably wouldn't have slowed until she had finished him off. She guessed she should be thankful for small favors, but she liked oral sex, loved giving head, and needed to give Walker something. He was always such an attentive lover.

A calloused hand stroked her cheek, then tilted her face up to meet his lips. Gentle, then rough, the sharp tingle and pull of her scalp told her he'd grasped a handful of hair. He released and then tightened again. There was a yank and a tingle as his mouth came crashing down on hers, bruising lips, tongues fighting, one hand landed on her still stinging bottom and squeezed. It hurt in such a good way. The ache was stoking her fire.

Then she did something totally out of character, Josie hopped and raised her legs to wrap around his waist, clinging to him as he plundered her mouth. Then he punished her ass as he held her immobile while he did it. Her core rubbed his shaft, and he shoved her legs down so he could turn her. Leaning over her, forcing her to bend over the bed, he patted her pussy from behind. The familiar spat announced how primed she was for him. She tensed when her cheeks were spread, placing the hard, fleshy cock in the crack.

Her nipple tightened more as he let the fleshy staff lay in her valley, allowing her to build on the anticipation of what he was going to do with his cock as he manipulated her nipple. She whined when Walker moved to the other nipple, rolling her to her side and spooning her, laying his cock back in its cradle. He worried her nipple with a forceful tug. Her sounds of want and distress merged in his intensity, causing her to clench her butt.

She rocked. The burn on her scalp merged with the occasional sharp swats he was giving her bottom, and her honey flowed down to pool at her anus. As if he expected that reaction, his hand moved downwards slightly to her now slippery back entrance. The puckered skin was tapped.

"Little girls who do not do as they are told, get to feel the sting of their man's hand, wherever he wants to put it. You're being such a good girl, don't fight me now, baby."

She rolled into him. He kissed her hard, stoking her need to get closer, her breasts smashed between them.

"Lift your leg over my hip." She did.

Thick, probing fingers traced her slit, coating the digits in her fluid before traveling forward to taunt her clit, then back through her stream of arousal to her dark entrance. With little fanfare, he circled then breached her anus.

"Yes."

She arched. Her moaned acceptance escaped her lips as her tight entrance was stretched, stimulated, and flexed as he plunged deep. Walker had been here before. His woman loved anal penetration, regardless of her mock resistance in the beginning. It was as though she had to pretend to protest this dark intrusion before she could surrender to its decadent pleasures. Today there was very little of that. Josie was oh so needy.

Two fingers were forced inside, their way aided by the new gush of arousal lubricating the path, drawing out another low cry. He plunged in again, and she held herself firmly in place to allow his fingers to do the job she wanted. Josie had told him that it hurt, but the harshness of the violation fed her need to be conquered, consumed. Her thoughts were only of completion.

He craved more. While leaving his fingers in her ass, he sat up, rearranged her slightly, putting each cheek on his corresponding thigh, then spread his legs. Her pussy and ass were exposed, and there was so much arousal honey that it dripped to the bed. He rammed himself into her weeping pussy.

"Fuck me. Hard," was all he said.

She immediately lifted up to come crashing back down on his hard, purple, blood-engorged cock, her ass cramming his digits back inside her as she bottomed out. After a few rounds of piercing her own body, she became fevered in her movements. She inched in different directions on each downward drop, trying and finally placed pressure on her clit as she compressed his gonads.

Suddenly she stopped, overtaken by muscle spasms that rippled and massaged his cock, her own fireworks display beginning. Walker assumed the cadence, elongating her pleasure and bringing himself to completion. They cried out together, their moans and panting merging, melding into one glorious experience. She loved the way he carefully exited her now well-used backside, then kissed her so gently.

The violent taking was over, and the funishment was done, the bruising treatment finished. Walker was suddenly gentle, reverent in his care of her. His kisses were caresses as he exited her pussy and placed her on her back.

"I'll be right back, sweetheart."

Josie felt so boneless she could only grunt her acknowledgment. The bed dipped within seconds, and a warm washcloth soothed her back entrance. The stickiness that was the combined essence of Walker and Josie's lovemaking, that unique scent that they produced together, was wiped away, leaving only the fulfillment being with him gave her.

"Did I hurt you?"

"Yes, well, kind of, but I'm amazed how much I loved it. I feel like I can't get enough."

"It was a punishment for being naughty and a reward for being mine."

"Hmm, then I must be naughty more often and allow you to declare your ownership." She rolled to settle in his arms and hissed. "But not this week."

"Dammit, I did hurt you. I meant it to hurt enough because I know you like that, but not in a lasting way. Rollover, let me look."

"What? No. If I am unduly sore tomorrow, you can look. I'm fine. Really, I loved it."

"Fair enough." He kissed her forehead, seeming to understand that she was tender everywhere. "Now go to sleep my naughty minx, we have a long day tomorrow."

Her answer was a breathy sigh and a snuggle closer to his chest. She licked his nipple and whined when he popped her ass again.

"Sleep."

Chapter 8

T he 6:00 a.m. alarm was unrelenting. Walker had woken Josie up in the wee hours of the morning in the sweetest way, kissing her in all the places he had been rough the night before, making tender love where he had been forceful earlier. Josie had expected to be sensitive in all the places he targeted the second time around, but his lovemaking covered all the spots and soothed them. She groaned and rolled over to pat the other side of the bed. It was cold and empty.

Well, if he has already left the bed, he won't notice if I sleep longer. It's his fault I'm so tired, anyway. Conscience absolved, Josie rolled over and fell back to sleep, comfy in her warm bed. Her next thought was of how chilly it was. In a drowsy haze, she reached for the cover and pulled it up. Just as she was settling back under the blanket, a familiar man's voice spoke in her ear, penetrating her sleep laden brain.

"Josie, time to get up, baby. Are you going to sleep the day away?"

"What?" was her groggy reply.

"You need to get dressed and get to work, sleepyhead. Your boss is a stickler for timeliness, and you're late. Anyone would have thought you had a wild night." Hot breath bathed her cheek and ear; the teasing tones made her warm through and through.

"I'm sleepy because some mean man woke me up and then kept me up until I was exhausted again. It can't be that late. Just a few more minutes." She tried to roll over, but half-way over, her partially exposed behind was patted, and the blanket was removed.

"Wrong. It's eight-thirty and time you were in the shower. I'll talk to the man who woke you up and tell him doubleheader nights are for the weekends. Now up you go." Another pat, not so gentle this time, landed on her derriere. Josie threw off the remaining vestiges of sleep and rolled to a sitting position on the bed.

"Daddy, have you at least made coffee?"

The air in the room seemed to be in a silent vacuum. Josie sucked in a deep breath, anticipation was thick. She looked up to Walker, her eyes wide. He grinned.

"I've done better than that; I brought you breakfast from the house. But you don't get it until you're ready to go, so if you don't want cold food and coffee, get a move on, baby."

Warm lips landed on her sleep dried ones. Josie was surprised they weren't sensitive today. Walker left the room and Josie, used to sleeping until the last minute before she had to leave, was well-practiced in the art of showering and dressing quickly, and in just over ten minutes, she dropped her pack in one of the extra dining chairs and sat as Walker set her plate before her.

"Wow, this is a lot of food. Are we sharing?"

"I've already eaten, but I'll finish what you don't eat. Waste not, want not. Hard working Daddy, remember?"

AS THEY DROVE THE MILE to the Clear Knight offices, a familiar pickup was in the front of the building. Piper's truck. Walker parked beside Piper and turned to watch Josie's reaction to their visitor and found her watching him, presumably for the same reason. They had not spoken to Piper since she had tricked them, over a week ago.

"How are you with Piper these days, honey? I can deal with her if you need me to. The thing is, we work the ranches as a team, so at some point, the whole crazy start of you working here must be dealt with, and we need to go on. Piper is the mother to my niece and the wife to my brother. Besides, we've been friends nearly all her life. But for today, how do you want to play this?"

"I thought it was you that was so angry with her. I know Piper, and I know how she is. Am I happy she manipulated us? Hell, no. Am I surprised? Not really. Did it seem to work out?" She shrugged.

"Did you just shrug at the question of whether this will work out or not?"

"Well, I don't have a crystal ball or anything."

"Sweetheart never doubt that you're mine, and I'm yours forever. We might work through some things and still have more to get through, more arguments and disagreements, but at the end of the day, we are a team in every way. Understand?"

"Yes. But I have issues that might not go away."

"Join the club, but you can't use that as an excuse to back away from us because I'm putting you on notice now, it will never work. I will hunt you down and paddle your rear end so soundly, you will wonder what type of issues you had that were more significant than your flaming ass."

"We have to talk about that stronger than average penchant you have to spank me. It has become more pronounced since I moved in."

"Yes, and when you settle down, so will the bottom warming. Until then, like a green cowboy trying to break his first horse, you are likely to sit gingerly often. It's up to you. Start talking, begin opening up about things that go on that bother you and your feelings, then I'll find less reason to light you up."

"So, if I find out you kept something from me, do I get to beat your butt?"

Walker laughed and opened his door. "Not a chance."

"What? What kind of fair is that?" She challenged.

"Did I ever say things were fair? Nope, and not equal either. Now let's go up and see Piper. We'll clear the air and go from there."

She started up the stairs, stopping after a few steps to turn and look at Walker. "I know, I'll withhold sex."

Walker laughed. "Yeah, you try that and see how it works out for you."

As they rounded the landing to the office, they nearly slammed into Jackson, talking on his phone. He ended his call and turned on the pair.

"Where the hell have you been? Do you know it's already nine in the morning?"

Josie seemed stunned for a moment before pulling herself to her full five feet six inches with two-inch heels on her boots. Still too short for significance, but obviously empowering to her.

"I'm sorry, I didn't see you on the schedule Jackson. Your phone isn't broken because you were just using it. There doesn't seem to be a fire, because I'm sure we'd have more indications than a clear blue sky. So, I am at a loss as to why you're so upset." Josie continued to her desk where Piper had been sitting, but when they entered, she had jumped up and stood off to the side.

The room was dead silent for about thirty seconds, then Jackson burst out laughing. When he settled down, he said, "I forgot your feistiness, Josie. I missed it." He nodded. "I did mean to call you, one of you, but I found myself coming anyway, so decided I'd stop. Sorry."

"Okay, now that that is done, what's up that you both came over?" Josie thought to say hello to Piper, but she decided the men could take care of the awkward transition back to being normal.

"Piper had some things to go over, but she was a little hesitant to come without reinforcements."

Walker nodded and started the coffee. "I get it. Piper, Josie and I did not appreciate the trick you played, leaving Josie left holding a very expensive bag and me in the lurch. We decided to try to make this work, and so far, we have, but that doesn't let you off the hook. I'm disappointed you chose that deceitful method to try to meet both our needs."

Josie broke in. "And yet, I can understand why you felt you needed to do it. If you had asked me if I would work for Walker, the answer would have been an immediate negative. In fact, I think we did have that conversation. Walker might have been different, but I was definitely still holding onto hurt when Walker didn't come back to be with me in Austin. I thought he'd moved on, emotionally, and there was no hope for us, which would have made me pathetic coming here for a job. But I still don't condone the method. Don't do it again."

"I promise. I just wanted the two of you to be happy, and you were both miserable, mostly because you had put that ravine between you. Am I forgiven?"

"Of course, you are. But I'm serious about not doing anything like that again." Josie offered Piper a weak smile and motioned her closer.

Piper walked into Josie's open arms. "I'm used to seeing something and making it happen. People do my bidding, and I expect it. I let my good intentions get in the way of good sense. I should have put your feelings first, not make you players in my plan. I am sorry, Josie."

"All is forgiven. Let's not talk about it again, okay?"

Piper nodded and looked over to Walker. "I'm sorry, Walker."

"I know, sweetheart." Walker turned to his brother. "Did you give her those extras from me?"

"Oh, God, did he ever."

"Then, all is forgiven." Walker opened his arms, and again, Piper walked into arms offering mercy. Walker leaned down to whisper something in Piper's ear. She smiled and nodded as he dropped a kiss on his sister-in-law's forehead and released her.

Walker made a beeline to the coffee pot. "Now, is this the whole issue, or do we have another problem to figure out today?"

"Nah, I've got another thing to discuss," said Jackson.

As the men talked horseflesh and cattle, Piper sat in the chair next to Josie's desk. "Looks like I'm going to need a small desk when I come to work. And I'll bring a laptop to leave here. I don't come often enough to do more. Can I see the new livestock and supplies inventory program you are transferring everything to?"

"Yep. I set it up and will be transferring all Clearwater Ranch data to it. I'm backing everything up from the old program, and if we ever get stuck, for a short time, we can go back to that one, but I don't think it will be necessary. Watch what this does."

For the next half hour, the two couples worked on ranching and then as Jackson and Piper rose to leave, Corey walked in, looking a little worried. Jackson raised his eyebrow in a query as he and Piper started to leave.

"We can talk later, Jackson. Tell me if that way works for the cattle, and we will implement it as the standard."

"Will do."

Walker turned to Josie. "Honey, we've run out of ground coffee. Could you grab some beans from the kitchen supply and grind us some? I'm feeling like it's going to be a long day."

Josie wondered what he was talking about because she had done that yesterday, but figuring he wanted her out of the room to talk to Corey instead of having her there, she agreed to go. She grabbed her pack with her tablet. Might as well do some organizing and noting what they were low on. It was a good way to see how efficient her inventory program was. If she could prove how good it was, maybe they could use it for things like bull sperm. That was so sensitive that it was kept by hand. She should show them they could print it off and always have it in hand as well. These Knight men were sure difficult sometimes.

Once out in the two kitchens supply area, she was scanning the items to adjust the inventory automatically when a rough hand landed hard on her shoulder from somewhere behind her, fingers dug into her skin. Her heart raced. Her breathing became tighter, and her chest felt like a weight was pressing. The person yanked her so hard her tablet flew out of her hand, pulling her back hard against his front. Her yelp of surprise was cut off by a dirty gloved hand over her mouth and one pressed tightly against her throat. Her hands instinctively went to her neck, clawing at the fingers holding her hostage, slowly squeezing the life out of her. The more she moved, the more he pressed her airway closed.

Panic approached overwhelming proportions in Josie's brain, but she forced herself to stay on the calmer side of chaos instinctively. Her body was still battling to retain that small bit of control when suddenly she was free of the pressure. The heated foul breath was gone, and so was her ability to hold on to her fear. She fell to her knees as her legs gave out, and the tears spilled from her fright-filled eyes. Her swollen throat allowed her to accompany her tears with a small hoarse cry of relief as she gulped in oxygen hungrily. Her autonomic system working to drag it in past swollen tissues. The release of her fear-fueled adrenaline high was loosening her chest.

Almost simultaneously, as voices surrounded her, worker voices, Sawyer's commanding voice cut through the others, but she didn't hear what he was saying. Walker had her folded in his arms, and before she knew it, he had checked her for injuries, cursed a lot, and scooped her up in his arms as though she weighed nothing. He strode into the main house, shouting orders and continued on into his room, all the while interspersing everything with the quiet question in her ear of whether she was hurt, and speaking out loud as he openly devised ways to kill Renfro.

Camille was a godsend. Her nursing skills were comforting to Josie. Once Camille and Josie convinced him she was going to be fine, they released Walker to return to the storage building and wait for the sheriff. It was nearly an hour before Walker and Sawyer walked in the house, having seen Renfro off to jail in the sheriff's truck. He was retiring this month after they elected a new sheriff, but the older gentleman wasn't easily fooled.

"Can you talk, baby? Need more tea? You warm enough?"

"Walker, man, she's doing okay. Chill. If you ask one question at a time, you find it gets answered." Sawyer shook his head.

"Fuck off. You'd be this upset if it were Camille."

"Yep. But it would still work better if you were calmer."

Josie put her hand out to Walker, who was pacing again. "I'm still shaky and jumpy, but I'm okay. Sit with me?"

They were right; he needed to calm the hell down and take care of his woman. He sat next to Josie and drew her into his side.

"I saw him walk into the building from the office window. I got down there as soon as I could, but it wasn't soon enough to stop him from hurting you. I'm so damn sorry."

Josie shivered, her voice raspy. "It was soon enough to stop him from killing me."

Another string of curses and Josie nearly crawled into his lap. Walker wasn't as good at nurturing as Sawyer, who was the intense daddy side of Camille the Nurturer, so he probably wouldn't think that was appropriate. He was an efficient and gentle daddy to her "tired of adulting" side, but she could use that Daddy now. She wanted to be done with adulting for just a little while. She sat fighting the tremors when suddenly she was sitting in Walker's lap, and a blanket was thrown over her.

"But you aren't like Sawyer. I'm okay."

"Nope, I'm not, but if my baby is shivering, her Daddy is holding her close. Don't ever doubt that I'm going to take care of you with or without the name, Daddy."

As an answer, she snuggled closer into him and fell asleep. When she woke, the sheriff was back again. She saw herself in a hallway mirror and gasped at the deep red and purple fingertip marks on her neck. After a bathroom stop and running a fast comb through her hair, Josie was back sitting next to Walker, who drew her in close. Camille brought her more tea and coffee for the guys.

"Ms. Rodriguez, can I ask what happened today?"

"I don't know. I went down to find something to do because Walker needed the office. I thought I'd update the original kitchen inventory." She stopped and turned to Walker. "My tablet flew out of my hands. Did you find it?" She coughed and tried to rub her throat but the pain stayed her hand. She released a cry of frustration. "And my backpack was left on the ground somewhere."

"We did baby, but it was broken. We'll fix it or get you a new one. I have your backpack." Josie nodded.

Since Walker and Sawyer were in the room with Josie, Camille left to tend to Colton. The sheriff looked at both Knight men and gave them a warning.

"Now, I'm going to interview Ms. Rodriguez, but if you boys don't think you can stay quiet, you need to find something else to do outside of this room. Do you get my meaning?"

Both men agreed. Walker's sounded more like a grunt than a yes, but the sheriff accepted it.

"Ms. Rodriguez? What happened after you entered the storage building?"

"I had barely started counting when I was grabbed by the shoulder and jerked around and my back was pulled tight to the man's body. Someone with bad breath was breathing next to my face. The person was taller than me but not like Walker and not as brawny. I tried to scream, but one hand was on my mouth and the other on my throat. I was trying, with little success I might add, not to panic because I couldn't breathe when someone pulled him off me."

"Did you know who it was?"

"No, but I thought I should know him. I was really just trying to breathe."

"And do you know Adam Renfro?"

"I didn't know that was his first name, nor do I know him, really, but I would recognize him."

"Ever exchange words with him?"

"A few."

"And yet you didn't recognize him when he was that close to you?"

Josie thought for a moment. "Honestly, no. It felt like someone familiar, someone I knew, but that was it. And I didn't worry that I couldn't see his face, because I was only thinking of getting away, of being able to inhale and exhale. You see, the man's body was leaning into me, hard, almost in a smothering way. I didn't see anything." Josie turned to the sheriff to stare him in the face. "When you're choking, when someone is pressing on your throat and squeezing, you think of nothing else but breathing."

"Fair enough, only Mr. Renfro states it wasn't him. He says you were panicking, and he was trying to calm you down."

"Well, Sheriff, I might consider that a possibility except for two things."

"And what are those things, Ms. Rodriguez?"

"I have never panicked before in my life until today when I couldn't breathe. When someone was cutting off my access to air."

"And the second?"

"When whoever arrived and pulled the man off me, I could immediately take in air. The pressure was off my neck, and I didn't feel like I was smothering to death. The panic receded quickly, and I fell to my knees on the ground. So, if the person who pulled him off me saw me crumble, then that was the moment the choking pressure was relieved."

"I see. But that doesn't say it was Renfro."

"No, but if the man who pulled him off says it was Renfro, then to me, that means it was him. Not because I identified him during the attack, but that action and reaction prove it."

The sheriff nodded. "Now I understand that it was Walker Knight who pulled Adam Renfro away from you, is that right?"

"So, I'm told. If Walker said so, then you can believe it."

"He did. He also said he had warned Renfro just this morning about being inappropriate with you, harassing, and intimidating. Is that right?"

"Again, I don't know. I know Walker was going to speak to Renfro. I also know that when Sawyer caught him yesterday in the act of trying to intimidate me, Sawyer issued a warning to Renfro."

"Okay, I'll talk to Sawyer, but why you? No offense, but you don't look dangerous, or like you would be a concern to a ranch hand, so why?"

Josie shrugged and shook her head. "Honestly? I don't know except what he told me. He said that a man who had worked on this ranch or at least a woman who had worked ranches, in general, should have gotten the job with Walker as his assistant. Because Walker and I are trying again to make our relationship work, Renfro said I was trying to get my hands on Knight money."

"And is there any reason he would think that?"

"None that I know of. I told him I'd worked here before. That I had worked on the ranch next door and had spent time with the Knights while working with Piper Knight. She was Gentry then. And I stayed here with Walker most of that time."

"As his girlfriend?"

"Yes."

"How long have you and Walker been in a relationship?"

"Off and on for about three years."

The sheriff stood. "Thank you, Ms. Rodriguez. I appreciate you speaking to me." He stood and grabbed his hat off the side table. Sawyer stood, and Walker allowed Josie to scoot off his lap that he had drawn her onto while she was talking, allowing him to stand as well. "And I appreciate how hard it was that you boys didn't say anything. Now, I've already talked to Walker, but Sawyer, I have a few questions for you, but I need to get back. Can we walk and talk?"

"Yep. I've got things I need to finish on the ranch, anyway."

Walker watched the men leave the family room, and he began his pacing again.

"Walker, we have things to finish today ourselves. I'm fine. I was shaken up, but I got a nap, tea, and comfort. Can we go back to the office?" When he hesitated, she pleaded. "Please?"

The rest of the day was spent in damage control. Josie decided she didn't want to leave the office. She said she was a little spooked still, and Walker understood that, but she didn't even want to eat lunch with the family and the ranch foreman, Cody Race. Okay, he thought, too soon. But when she hesitated to leave the office to go home, Walker knew he had to address it.

"Know what happens when a person falls off a horse?"

"They hit the ground?"

"Cute. Yes, they hit the ground, but more than that, their security takes a hit. They begin to wonder about the safety of the horse and them on it. Then, if unaddressed, they begin to question the safety of all horses."

"Okay, but why are you telling me this?" She shook her head. "This is not the same thing, Walker. I was attacked. Renfro wanted to kill me or at least make me pass out. He wanted me to be scared."

"So, are you just going to give him that power? You're going to let him intimidate you even while he's in jail?"

"You don't understand. It isn't like I want to; it's just a powerful feeling."

"Yes, and like the person who falls off their horse, you have to get back into the normal fray quickly, or your fears will grow and overtake you."

"Walker..."

"Grab your backpack and let's go." She did. Walker kissed her but kept her moving with his hand splayed on her lower back to encourage forward movement. He propelled her to the main house and through the kitchen door. She was slow traveling the whole way.

"I'm going to wash up," Josie said the minute she hit the kitchen door. Walker was waylaid by Jackson at the same time. Walker hesitated and watched his girl quickly disappear into the house.

Everyone was sitting down to eat when Walker noticed Josie hadn't returned. "You all go ahead. I'll just go grab Josie."

After combing the house in search of her, Walker was about to give up until he thought of one last place to check. There was a place between the wardrobe in his bedroom and the far wall. The only way you could see it was if you walked over to that side of the room and looked in that direction. Lily and Eli had both hidden there once when they'd been up to mischief, and Sawyer was looking for them. Josie knew it was there. It was safe.

Entering with the pretext of searching for a clean shirt, he turned, seemingly by accident, and there she was, curled up in a ball, tears streaming down her face. It broke his heart.

"Come on, baby, let's go home."

"I'll just wait until you've had dinner."

"How about I go get us some dinner, and we take it home?"

"Could we?"

"Yeah, honey, we can. Wait here. I'll be back."

"Mmhmm."

Making their excuses, he got a casserole dish and made it up for their dinner. Waving to their concerned family, he carried the dish in a tote and led Josie to the truck to drive back to her cottage. She preferred calling it a "cottage" to "the cabin." He spent the rest of the evening putting her at ease. She was afraid of being alone, but also afraid of anyone else. Not anyone in particular, really, because he did ask. She was just worried someone would jump her again, and this time she wouldn't survive.

His woman took every bump in the road as a challenge. What made this different from those other times was that she had, for the first time in her adult life, been unable to help herself enough to get by. She was unable to save herself. She could have died without ever being in control of that situation. She was almost manic about that now. Like she didn't trust her own instincts anymore.

The first night, she locked the front door twice, locked, unlocked to check if it was locked, and then locked again. She checked the windows behind him, made sure the sensor light worked by tripping it several times, and she slept in clothes. She had always enjoyed sleeping in the nude, or nearly nude, but no longer. She was dressed enough that if there was a fire, she could get out without worrying about her state of covering. Her lockbox was just under her side of the bed, moved from the closet, and she pulled out the bat she had that had lived in the closet until now.

"Josie, I know this is to make you feel secure, but honey, you are safer than you were. Renfro is gone. In jail. Charges are going to be pressed. Do not worry. Please, relax."

"I can't. I will, after a few days. Honest. I just need this right now." Walker knew deep down that it wasn't going to work that way, but he'd give her a couple of days before he took over.

Chapter 9

J osie sat hard in the office chair and then popped up in painful remembrance of her sore bottom. She shook her head at the reality of her world. She took a quick look to make sure none of the Knight men or their foreman, Cody Race, were lurking. Cody subscribed to the Knights' ideology on dealing with their women when found out of the bounds of acceptability, and she rubbed her soreness for a bit.

If she didn't love the way her body responded to his dominance, she might have talked herself out of letting Walker swat her ass. The truth was, she was discontent when he hadn't shown he adored her in every way, including making love to her. Josie came even harder with her butt burning. She was the one watching the cowboy movies when the man flipped the woman over his lap for getting into fixes they knew better than to do or disobeying their man's rules.

"You too? Better not let the guys see you," said Camille with a chuckle.

Josie sat gingerly in her cushioned seat and grinned back. "All clear. I checked."

Josie threw her the cushion she had in her bottom drawer. "I wouldn't make you sit on the hardwood although I've had to do it before. What is it with these guys?"

Camille shrugged. "I used to ask that too, but I kind of understand now. They take getting used to, like Walker hates a real brat, but Jackson likes it. Sawyer doesn't really care, but if you brat him, he will always address it."

"So, it's according to their personalities. Walker doesn't suffer a fool, and he had practically drawn and quartered one of the hands when they argued with him when he knew they were wrong. He lets me argue all I want, but if I lose, he pulls out the paddle." Josie gave a mock shudder. "And I like to argue. It's fun, gets the blood pumping, you know? I want my own way and have gotten good at battles of the wit. Unfortunately, Walker likes being the boss and seems to know how to give me just enough rope to hang myself. Not a good combination."

"Sawyer doesn't want me to do anything that might be unsafe. His idea of unsafe is taking off the cotton wool when I leave the house." She smiled dreamily, "I have never felt so protected and loved as I do with Sawyer. I know he will do everything in his power to make me happy. I know what it's like without that. What's a little spanking next to what I get from that man?" Camille grinned. "And the sex..."

"Yep, that is definitely a huge plus."

"So, I'm meeting Piper in town for lunch soon. Wanna come with me?"

"Camille, I can't. I have so much to do here."

"Okay, well, what if I ask Piper to meet us here? She can bring lunch with her." Camille's eyes flashed with an idea. "I know, let's go down to the creek. A long time ago, the boys' daddy built a cedar table so they could have picnics by the stream. It's so nice. Come on."

"No, I'm good. I really do have work to do."

"Look, I'm saving you another conversation about taking care of yourself because Walker has told Sawyer he's worried about you and that you hardly eat these days. He even mentioned feeding you. Making it part of a sexy time so you would eat."

"No way!"

"Yep. This way, I can say we had lunch, and you ate while getting sunshine and fresh air. He'll be ready to do your bidding tonight, if you know what I mean, as a reward."

"Just the three of us?"

"Yes. I'm leaving the baby with Sawyer this afternoon. Please?"

Josie hesitated, but Camille was right. Walker was worried about her since the episode last week with Renfro. Her throat had hurt for a few days, and the bruising looked impressive, but being in a group, even just eating with the Knights, caused anxiety. This would be her way of proving that she wasn't afraid any longer, even if it was only a half truth.

At first, she worried that some unknown assailant would attack her. But once Cody came back full time, having taken a few weeks off to settle in with his new fiancée, no one dared to take a step out of line. She relaxed in that knowledge. There was still a hyper-vigilance she hadn't experienced since her mother had allowed one of her benevolent friends to visit the trailer. It was rare, but the feeling of slime and fear wasn't something one could easily forget.

Having the respect of the ranch hands was important, but at first, it was expected that they simply show deference to her position on the ranch and to the Knight family. Josie appreciated that the hands who didn't know the whole story would think it was her fault somehow, but Monday, when Cody came back, he laid down the law. She was called ma'am, which she was still getting used to, and there was not a snide remark among them, well, not to her face, anyway. And that sufficed for now.

Josie felt petty demanding they not be rude to her, but any other work environment demanded that and more. Walker had been livid and protective. It took him until Cody returned before he was able to do other work without it coloring every response. That was Walker, Sawyer, and Cody's ball game.

Trying to get Walker to unwind and let go of the issue helped her take herself out of the thick of things, she could relax more than she had expected, but still, she was touchy. And her heart raced at every little unexpected movement. She almost felt paranoid. Logically, Josie knew Renfro was out of the picture. They had even moved him to the county jail, nearly thirty miles away, but that niggling fear remained.

Josie tried to hide her jumpiness. Keeping things from Walker was not easy for her, and for the most part, she thought she had been successful. Josie frowned; she had failed miserably. She had convinced him so well that he had her lie across his knee last night when he caught her eating lunch again in the office yesterday. It didn't help that the lunch consisted of some cheesy crackers and a supercharged caffeine drink.

"You're losing weight." His accusing tone had stopped her for a moment.

"You're imagining things. I'm the same weight I was before taking this job."

"Okay, how much did you weigh?"

"110." The number shot out of her mouth before she had thought to drop the number a few pounds, just in case.

"So, let's go weigh you now."

"No way. It's a different scale."

"How do you know it doesn't weigh the same as your home scale?"

"Because I tested it."

Walker smiled, and Josie groaned. "And what did you weigh?"

Josie looked at Walker for a moment, wondering if she could get away with subtracting a few numbers but decided she'd better stick to the truth. "109."

"Okay, on this scale, 109 is your normal, albeit lean number. Let's go see what you weigh now."

Josie knew there was a possibility that she had lost a pound or two, but that couldn't hurt, right?

Walker looked like thunder. Josie had long learned that he took on that stone face when he thought there was a possibility that she wasn't safe. Health equated safety, and if he thought she'd lost weight, and she had, well, there was little hope for getting around that.

"I'd rather not. There are some things a girl doesn't like to share, and her weight is one of them, Walker. You should know that." Good, taking the offensive had always worked with others.

"Too bad. Now either you walk into the bathroom under your own power, or I take you over my shoulder with appropriate addressing of your disobedience."

"Fine, but I'm doing this under protest. And I can't be disobedient. I'm not your child."

Walker had smiled then. "No, but you are my employee." He was enjoying this. "I understand the sacrifice you are making for my peace of mind."

"Oh, shut up. You know I wouldn't do this if you weren't right to keep me focused on being safe." Josie felt militant, and he was again frowning heavily but said nothing more until she had climbed on the scale.

"107," he announced.

And that had been the end of her sitting well for the rest of yesterday and today. Well, this morning, at least. It had been a challenge because Walker said he was "freshening" her memory to eat a good lunch.

"There is absolutely no excuse when one is provided for you." He said as he placed her fruit and yogurt in front of her.

He was right, of course, it was just that usually there were a few others at the table because the guys were always talking work at lunch. She was skittish about not knowing them well enough to trust them yet. Even though her mind said very logically that she was behaving anything *but* logically, it was her anxiety, and it was real. So, when she had decided not to show up for lunch yesterday, even though he had warned her there would be consequences, that had been the last straw for her over-protective man. He understood all he could but unless you experienced the stomach seizing and the pressure building in a group of men, you couldn't actually know.

The final ache was really gone now, but her poor bottom deserved some pampering. She had endured a long, hard spanking with Walker's hand. His fingerprints could be felt even in the night when he woke her up to have sex again. Piper said Jackson didn't lecture when he spanked, but Walker did, and that's what broke her. He really cared about her. She was a wounded cuddle toy right now, and she needed some TLC.

"I told you how precious you were to me, baby, and I can't have you treating my girl this way. I can get you help if you need it to work through some of the games your mind is playing, but you have to eat enough and sleep enough." Evidently, waking her up for sex didn't stop her from getting enough sleep. Josie did grin about that.

He didn't know that his words had hit a chord deep inside that had been sheltered from anyone for so long, that Josie had almost forgotten it existed. The spot he hit carried the belief that not everyone was out for themselves. She always tried not to be self-centered, but until last night, while Walker had landed his big paw on her naked ass and crooned his affections, she hadn't realized she believed everyone else was out for personal gain. Once the light had shone on her erroneous belief, it was all she could see.

Walker really cared. How could she not do as he asked to help him not worry about her? That is why Josie agreed to go on an outdoor lunch excursion. It was why she decided to walk into the stables with the two Knight women and why she rode to the stream with them, trying her hardest to push her insecurities and anxieties to the far back of her mind. The lunch of deli meats, olives, cheeses, and pickles with stone ground mustard, veggies, and fresh-baked bread was the best sandwich she'd ever tasted.

"Mmm, this is an incredible sandwich."

Piper grinned. "It is, and I have to limit myself to once a week, or I'd be as big as a house."

"Maybe you should eat one a day, Josie," said Camille. "Then you won't have to worry about losing weight."

"Walker?" asked Piper.

"Yep," sighed Josie. "I lost two pounds, and Walker wasn't impressed."

"Women's weight fluctuates," said Piper.

"True, but I really haven't been eating well, and I'm a little under the ideal weight limit."

"How does he know?" asked Camille.

"He made me look it up last night before he roasted my rear."

Piper shook her head. "I hate it when they win."

"My ass sure hated it." The horses were restless for some reason, and Josie, who loved horses dearly, stood to check on them, but Piper stopped her when they settled right back down.

"They probably had something fly across their path. They sound fine now."

"Probably," agreed Josie.

"Okay, so what's happening with that Renfro character?" asked Piper.

"Don't know. Evidently, the state has taken over the charges, but what I do know is he is not allowed back on the ranch, or within 500 feet of me. Can we talk about something else?"

The conversation turned to other subjects but soon, Josie stood to go back. "I do have a job, and Walker will wonder why I'm gone so long."

"Probably, but he won't worry if you're with us," offered Camille.

"Maybe, but I need to go back, nonetheless."

Josie was the first to pull her horse, Crescent, away from the spot she'd left him to graze. Grasping the reins, she noticed he was a bit skittish, causing her to look around for a reason, but finding none, she started to mount again. As she was about to swing her right leg over, the gelding spooked for real. He did an odd hop and side shuffle, dancing away from her and then from the bushes when he got close, only to turn and race forward a distance. Josie yelled out in pain as she dropped to the ground.

Piper ran after the horse, and Camille put on her nurse's cap.

"What happened?" asked Camille as she took stock of the situation.

"Ow, damn that hurts. I mean, really hurts." Her hiss and assorted mutterings and moans attested to the fact that she was very much in pain. "It's burning like the devil and feels like I nearly yanked it from my body."

"Well, you nearly did, in all practicality. Pretty sure you've pulled and hyper-extended the tendons and ligament of your left arm. Good thing you're right-handed."

"Camille," said Josie through clenched teeth, "no perky sunshine moments, okay. This hurts too bad."

"Oh, right, sorry." Camille took her overshirt and tied Josie's left arm tight to her body for support.

Piper walked grimly toward her companions with the horse in tow. She held up the horse's tail. "Nettles in his tail, too many to be an accident, and under his saddle. You would not have been able to ride if these were under the saddle coming out. Besides, she was freshly tacked up."

Piper and Camille exchanged a look. "Ride back with me, and Piper can handle Crescent. I'll go slow, but Piper, you call ahead and get Walker ready to take her into the clinic."

Climbing on the back of the horse even when standing on a log and both women helping made it excruciatingly painful, but Josie was finally in the saddle.

Josie said nothing on the way back, just the occasional moan when they were jarred more than normal. Walker came up to Camille's horse and helped Josie down, careful not to spook the horse. Once they were away from the animals, Walker turned his accusing face to Piper.

"What the hell happened?" Josie whimpered. "It's okay, baby, we're going to the clinic."

Josie continued through her clenching jaw. "It's not her fault or Camille's. Something was wrong with the horse's saddle. Let Piper tell you."

Piper filled him in briefly. He turned to Camille, "Will you call and tell the doctor what happened, so he knows when I get there?"

"Yep. Miss the potholes as much as possible because until she gets some pain pills, she is going to be in unbearable pain."

"Got it."

Piper returned with Josie's pack from the saddle horn. "Thanks, Piper. Hey," said Walker, "I was out of line, and I'm sorry."

"I've lived with you Knights my whole life. Nothing I can't handle, but Walker, those horses sounded like they were spooked while we were having lunch. Because they settled down quickly, we didn't think anything of it. I don't think this was an accident. Now, get her to the clinic."

"Right." He turned and carefully helped her walk, but when it appeared too much for her to do, he slung the pack on his shoulder and gently scooped her up into his arms.

CAMILLE AND WALKER put Josie to sleep in his bed. He was keeping her in the house with him and with quick access to Camille. They had more resources in the main house than they had at the cabin. Josie tried to complain, but the pain medicine kicked in hard, sending her off to sleep with the fairies. She was going to need the pain meds and muscle relaxers for at least a week. Walker had no intention of her leaving his bed for much of that time.

Entering the family room, Walker looked at his brothers and their wives. The two couples had worried expressions, and it was obvious that they had some concerns. So, did he.

Sawyer asked, "Josie asleep?"

Walker nodded. "Doc said it wasn't as bad as he had feared. I guess she held onto the reins too long when Cascade lurched forward but not so long that she did permanent damage, thank God. It will be a month before her arm will work much and longer before she will be operating normally. He said the tendons and ligaments were not snapped, but they were definitely hyper-extended. She'll need physical therapy but not for a few weeks. She's going to hate that." He turned to address the women. "Piper, can you and Camille tell me the story again?"

By the time the story had been retold, Camille asked what everyone was thinking. "Who would do this? I mean, on this ranch, with everyone working in twos at least, who could slip off, sabotage poor Cascade and get back unnoticed?"

Jackson spoke, his words sounding harsh. "It was lunch for most of the ranch. Anyone could have slipped away from the meal or shown up late, and no one would have noticed. Or it would hardly have been noticed."

"Or they weren't following ranch rules in partnering up. We need to try to figure out which it is. We should see who ate first and last, who walked out of their meal, or never walked in." said Walker.

Sawyer spoke up, "Who would have known that Josie was riding Cascade?"

Walker answered his brother. "She always rides him if she has a choice. She's fallen in love with him, and he is pretty damned fond of her, too. Anyone who works the stables or the barns would know."

"Or has seen her riding," added Camille.

Piper, who had been fairly quiet, said, "Do you think some-one is targeting her or was it just a random prank that went wrong? There are a few young guys still wet behind the ears we recently hired on."

"No idea at this point," said Jackson. "But I pray it *was* a prank because there is nothing good going to happen if it wasn't. Unfortunately," continued Jackson ominously, "Until we know for sure what happened and why, you two and the children are going to need to stay in places where you aren't alone." Piper opened her mouth, and Jackson gave her a with-ering look as he held up his hand to stave her objections. "Hear me out, woman. You drive straight to work and straight home. If either of you needs to be anywhere but the house or office, you do it with someone. We work in pairs for safety, you will too, for now."

Piper spoke with a hint of disdain. "You do remember that there were three of us together when whoever did this was perpetrating the crime. Right?"

"Yes, but Piper, my love, you are making my case."

"No, the point I'm making is if they want to do some damage, they will. The responsible party had no trouble performing his act today. We could have had five ladies, and it would have happened. We just have to be smart." Piper turned to Camille. "Do you have bear spray?"

"Nope, but I can go get some tomorrow."

Sawyer's daddy voice was intense. "Under no circumstances will you leave this house without telling me. Am I clear, Camille?"

"Sawyer, I have things to do."

"Understood. I can assign someone to follow you around, just in case."

"You're just so... so," Camille looked up into her husband's hard face, and her words faltered. "Nothing." Her shoulders slumped in defeat. "But it isn't fair."

"I agree, but safety is not negotiable. It's late, and we need to go to bed. We have a long day tomorrow."

Piper scooped up her little Janine from the playpen in the corner. Jackson and Piper were whispering in irritated tones as he took their daughter from Piper and led the way to the truck. Walker wished everyone good night, but he was still concerned that his girl was in danger, and he didn't know where it was coming from except it was internal. He couldn't stand that thought. He would rout them out, and then he'd... no, he couldn't go to a dark place where he fantasized about killing the asshole who dared mess with his woman. Not now, Josie needed him.

He'd placed her so her left arm was away from him, but it wasn't the side she normally slept on. He couldn't bear to think about hitting her shoulder and arm in the night; however, he couldn't leave her alone either. It was going to be a long night.

Chapter 10

Healing was a slow, boring, irritating process that brought out the snarky in her. If Josie had felt better, her butt would have been stinging all the time. Josie knew she was moody. She felt it, embraced it even. She had gone back to her cabin after five days. It was all she could take of a hovering man that mixed sternness with nursemaid behaviors. The combination was too tough to deal with for long. She would argue, and he would start to put her in her place, but Walker would then remember that she was hurt, close his mouth and walk away. Walker blamed himself. Josie was never so frustrated in every way possible as she was now.

The minute she moved back home, she felt relieved. Then came the loneliness and anxiety at being by herself most of the day. As had become his habit since she'd left the main house, Cody stopped to check on her as he was passing the cabin on the way to another pasture or chore. Josie nearly had a heart attack the first time. When she found it was just him, she chewed his ass.

Cody, being the good soul that he was, simply tightened his hold on his hat, scrunched his lips fiercely to keep his mouth shut, and left her still spouting. Ten minutes later, Walker came striding through the door and put her to bed for a nap.

"I'm not a child, Walker, I'm just hurt and frustrated and maybe a little short-tempered. Need I remind you that I'm not Camille and you are not Sawyer?"

"Oh, I think you are very much like Camille right now and Piper when she is in a mood. And I am very much like either of my brothers when it comes to taking care of their women."

"But Cami loves the intense coddling. I'm not that woman."

"Then prove it, because I don't believe you," he shot back at her. "You were a scared, petulant child this morning when Cody came by. You were more than that, you were downright rude, and that is not going to happen on my watch, no matter how frustrated you are. It is out of character, but you've had time to pull it together. You have plenty of pain pills and all the coddling you will accept."

"I'm going slowly mad doing nothing, can't you see that?"

"What I see is you have withdrawn into your Josie Only Club, and you want everyone to leave you to it. If they don't agree that it is horrible and let you get away with mouthy, bratty behavior, then too bad for them. I've seen you do this before to push others away. It is either a calculated move or an unconscious response, but the end goal is to create an atmosphere of self-protection, so you don't risk showing your vulnerability. It's why you weren't having lunch at the main house anymore. We've got to deal with the reasons you are afraid."

Josie sat in a sulk, but her guilt was doing a good job of making her feel even worse, except she couldn't let go of the ill-tempered behavior. "I'm sorry," she said crabbily.

"Nope. You'll apologize when you're in a better mood. Now, I don't want to spank your sexy ass, but if you keep this up, you will soon have something real to rant and rave about. You get me, girl?"

Josie was immediately contrite because deep down, she didn't want to treat Cody badly. It was that the contrary part of her was still very much in control. She ignored Walker and turned away only to screech her surprise as the sound and sting hit at the same time. He'd slapped her thigh.

"Try that again? With words this time."

"Yes, I get you," she spoke through clenched teeth.

Why didn't Walker just spank her so she could release the whole mess she was holding onto tightly? It was a stress reliever, and since they always had sex afterward, she would be lighter and satiated. But she categorically refused to ask. He knew she craved the release. If he wanted to help her, he would just take over.

"Good enough for now." Josie deflated when he missed her cue. "Now we need to work you through being skittish every time something as innocent as a visitor comes knocking on the door."

"What do you know about it? You've never had this gnawing type of anxiety. You're a man with plenty of money and power. You were born into the whole wonderful life scenario, so you've never felt like you had to worry about anything. You were never vulnerable, looked down on, ridiculed."

"Maybe, maybe not, but I do know how to work a skittish animal past its fear. We simply expose the creature often but in small bites until he is desensitized to the item or event or whatever. Then it no longer gives him a fright."

"So, I'm a farm animal, am I? Thanks for that edifying classification. And what are you planning to do, expose me to assholes that you employ until one of us gets over either our fixation or sensitivity?"

"You're putting up a wall to rebuff others, so they stay away."

"I'd say it was a good strategy. Look, no one has attacked me in days!"

Walker raised his voice in frustration. "You don't have to deal with the issues at hand if you block them out. The elephant in the room must be addressed, Josie."

"So now you're saying I'm the problem, the big *fat* problem. Very odd indeed since you just jumped on my butt for losing two fucking pounds."

Josie spat out the bitter words before she'd processed what she had said to her lover. The man who had bent over backward to do whatever she had wanted since she'd been hurt didn't deserve this treatment, and she knew it. As much as she loved him for it, she hated the lack of control she felt when Walker shined a light on her problem and the insecurity it brought with it. Violently hated it.

Walker stood solid and firm with eyes shining his love even though he stood immobile as stone. "Yeah, baby, I am. I'm saying it's time to deal with your thinking."

She looked away from the painfully tight lips and the frustration that was growing into something akin to anger before her eyes. Moving away from Walker, Josie needed something to break her mood before it destroyed her relationship and broke her. She needed to get her control back or some semblance of control. It was vital.

"I want to help you find him," she said quietly and firmly.

"Excuse me?" The change of conversational direction took him by surprise. "Find who?"

"Him. The person who hurt Crescent."

"You mean, hurt you."

"Yes, and me, but I was worried about my horse. I knew I'd survive."

Walker grunted. His response was stated matter-of-factly. "You aren't going anywhere but back to Doc when it's time and physical therapy after that."

"And the office."

"No, not for a while."

"Dammit, Walker. You're doing just what he wants. The person who did this gets his way. I'm not in the office or wandering the ranch with or without you now because of this. I'm not with anyone. I'm here, alone, vulnerable. A target."

Walker looked up from the floor, as her words penetrated. She held her tongue when the word lonely wanted to tumble out. Josie was not going to admit she had gotten used to her office and bed companion to the point that it was lonely without him near all day. Nor admit to herself or anyone that she was falling so hard for Walker that she might not survive without him.

Josie couldn't give him that power. Not because she didn't trust him, but because she didn't dare risk becoming more vulnerable. Her defenses were low enough. Nor would she admit that she'd begun to enjoy other people. Watching the Knights work together, as she had since arriving back on the ranch, showed her how much they relied on each other, and how they were responsible for things jointly. They depended on one another to get a job done. She had begun to depend on Walker.

The issue came up when there were so many others she didn't trust, didn't feel safe with. Josie's walls couldn't go up and down like an electronic gate.

"Okay, look. We're going to sit at the table, and I'm going to make us lunch. During which time you will tell me what is really going on. You've begun to talk in circles, riddles, and I'm a little worried about what you plan to do if I don't agree to let you sleuth the miscreant out with us."

"It's not that," denied Josie as she sat in one of the dining chairs. "I can't give up control, is all. And I don't trust easily. Now, with this, I can't risk it outside of you five and Cody."

"Can't or don't want to?"

"Both?"

Walker nodded and worked quietly for a short time before continuing. "Safety and health, those are the only things that I have mandated as things you cannot ignore. Right?"

She shrugged. "I guess."

"I'm not Jackson, who looks for reasons to discipline Piper, not that she doesn't deserve it more often, but she loves it. It works for her. I'm not Sawyer that wants Camille to be sweet, and feisty is okay too, so long as he can address it. Curse words are a no go with him as are things like leaving without talking to him. Of course, all that falls into his definition of Daddy play."

"I don't go in for bratting, but I love sensual play, and so do you. The only thing I discipline for is ignoring your safety or your health. And our experiment on asking for help when needed. Daddying you is a pleasure and a bedroom thing or when it's a discipline thing. I nurture but not like Sawyer. Do you think differently?"

"Yes, you have chewed me out for being mouthy."

"With other things, maybe, but not by itself. You can't curse me, but in general, I don't care."

"No. You're right, but I don't do things that are dangerous, well, not on purpose. And I take good care of my health."

"Usually, I would agree, which is why you don't get many over my knee sessions, but sometimes you think something is safe when it isn't. I think you want to do it, so you say it's safe. Looking for the idiot who caused your accident is not safe, and you won't do it. Talking about making you a target like Piper did? That would do it. I'd be slapping that ass every day. We don't know the motivation behind him sabotaging the horse, and you are injured. Two good reasons that it would never be safe for you to go on a modified manhunt. I wouldn't be taking care of you if I let you go in search for an unknown culprit. And, unless I make you eat, like now, you tend to skip over meals lately, after the first incident with Renfro and now this."

Walker placed two bowls brimming with tomato soup and then a plate of sandwiches with thick slices of ham and melted cheese in the center. They ate in companionable silence for a short while before Josie spoke, after eating nearly half of what he put before her. She slid it away from her. He raised his brow but said nothing.

"I know what you're saying, but sometimes I get so anxious, so angry or both, about the whole thing. I just want to take control. I must have control of my life. You want it for yourself, and I'm no different. I'm not proud of it, but really, I'm not upset about that being a huge part of my makeup. What happened with Cody today, I do feel bad about that, but in some ways, I'm still angry. I'm steaming that in an area that I thought was ultra-safe people wise, this incident quickly showed me it wasn't."

"It's my fault."

"It isn't, Walker, but I'm interested in hearing why you think so."

"I employed Renfro. I probably employ the man who caused your accident. I mean, it could have been a neighbor kid, but..." He shrugged. "And I brought you here."

"But there are no homes for a long stretch of land from this place, so neighbors are likely out. And school is in session, so again, isn't possible. I was new, Renfro was resentful, and he took it out on me. You brought me here because you and I agreed. No kidnapping or coercion was to blame."

"You're right." Walker polished off the last sandwich and stared at his empty plate. Josie offered the second half of her sandwich. He smiled and took it.

Josie was pensive. "You know, I did wonder if he applied for that job?"

"Your job? No. I mean we *did* have that conversation where he said he should be either mine or Sawyer's second, but that was it. We share a second and that's Cody. We don't need more. You are my second because you are good at this and we are a team. Two people applied to the posting before this one. Jackie Marsh from a ranch some distance away, and Sherry Collins. She was from somewhere north of here. She would have had to relocate as well."

"So, you didn't know them?"

"Oh, Jackie went to the same school and is from around here, but she was younger than I was, and I never really knew her during those years except in passing. Never met Sherry Collins before the interview."

"Okay, well, it wouldn't be sour grapes with them, then."

"Nope."

"What about, like Camille, someone is mad I'm dating you?"

"But they aren't. I mean, I wasn't Sawyer, hound dogging it everywhere until I lost interest altogether. I have only dated you since we met. I never was inclined to look elsewhere. You?"

"Is it bad that I have? Only a couple of creepy dates, but that was a while ago, too. I guess someone could have hacked into the dating site but..."

"Wait, are you telling me that you used a dating service?"

"Yep."

"After we dated?"

"Well, not during that time, but during the first break, yeah. I figured since I had left Piper and she was going to be in your family, it was a lost cause."

"After I educated you on keeping yourself safe, you opened an account for an online dating service and went out with men from there? Men you had never met before?"

"Yes. I wasn't with you then. What are you upset about? I was careful."

"How could you be careful if you went out with men you didn't know? That is all the more reason to never let you go."

"Okay." She didn't want to leave.

His granite face almost looked like it would explode, causing Josie to experience some trepidation. Then he turned serious eyes to her and said in a deceptively quiet voice, "I'll work this out and see if you can do some small things to help and still not break the house rules."

"There are rules too?"

"Of course."

"Then, you have to abide by them too."

"I already do. Now go take a nap, and if you know what's good for you at all, you will not argue." He mumbled almost to himself as he stood to clear the table. "My woman does not go out with men she hasn't met before." He turned back around to stalk back to the table.

Josie automatically opened her mouth but then quickly closed it again. "All right. I get it. I promise never to do it again." She hid her smile at that. Of course she wouldn't. She would be with him. "Will you go back to work?"

"Will you be afraid?"

"No, I'll be fine."

"Okay, I'll go work on the second-round breeding schedule. You call me when you get up."

"If I need something, I will."

"No, not if you need something. When you wake up."

"Fine, when I wake up." She huffed her response. Walker just shook his head.

He waited until she had crawled into bed before he left. Josie knew she had dodged the bullet on that little disclosure. She wouldn't be so careless again. They were going to find whoever had done this to her, figure out why he did it, and then Josie could relax and get on with the business of living. She hoped.

This person tried to take from her what she was ready to admit she loved: Walker, his life, his home, his family. Josie had turned off any possibility that love would be in her future the last time she couldn't call Walker back. She knew she was capable, but loving someone gave up some of your control. Until today, that was not something Josie was ready to do to the extent that loving a man like Walker would demand. Josie felt no guilt. In fact, she felt a little excited at the hunt ahead. She was taking back her life, her control and was going to win, and she was going to do it with help.

"I WASN'T TOTALLY AWAKE yet."

"I call bullshit, girl. You were awake and texting on your phone but couldn't, or chose not to, use it to call me and say you were up. That has just earned you a blistered ass. I'm willing to give you some latitude, but I need you to follow my orders."

"Your orders?"

"My orders. When I say do something, I need to know you will do it because even if you don't agree, you know I don't issue them idly. It's for your benefit, and it's to that end, and only that end, that I give expectations. Now, it will be your rear end that will pay the price."

"Okay, wait. Now please explain to me how it was going to benefit me that I called you when I woke up? I didn't need anything."

"Yes, but I was going to get you to the office so you could piddle around in there a while. Not going to happen now, and not sure tomorrow either since you are going to see Doc and then have your first physical therapy session. I think that might be enough for one day."

"Oh. Why didn't you just say that?"

"Trust. You've got to learn to trust me, Josie, and evidently, I'll have to train you to do it. This is how I train. Now, let's get this over with."

"But... I'm hurt."

"Yes," he answered seriously, "so you had better lay over the bed for the best support."

"No, that's not how a spanking is supposed to be given."

Walker laughed. "No? Well, then I'll have to do something else to teach you to mind me when I'm specific, huh? Strip, little girl."

"Wait, it's hard to take my things off. I don't want to struggle again. Going to the bathroom is crazy difficult."

His laugh settled into a grin that spread broadly over his face. His eyes danced, making her wary of that devilish look. "Then don't wear pants. I can help you right now, though." And in a flash, her pants and undies, that were not of the enticing variety, had been lowered to the floor, and the rush of cooler air gave her a chill. She shrieked at the embarrassment of her sudden exposure.

"What are you doing?" The sound of a determined hand meeting soft, unsuspecting backside cheeks hit her ears before the ensuing blaze was felt on her bottom. "Ow. What was that for?"

"For me. I couldn't resist my urges. Now lay across the bed, feet on the floor. I want access to your bottom, but you need to be as comfortable as you can be." Josie hesitated. "If you take any longer, I'm likely to swat your ass more."

"But..." Another swat resounded throughout the room. "Okay, okay." She stood rubbing. He appeared to be preparing for another swat, and that put her in motion, trying to position herself while he pulled out a bag he'd thrown into the closet.

"Get comfortable. I have something to help you remember you are mine, and I protect what's mine. I also remind my girl if she's having trouble believing I am doing the best I can for her. Following my instructions is the first stage of trust. I am going to take care of you, and you are going to let me. This will help."

Walker rubbed Josie's bottom in circles, kneading the plump flesh, patting it as though he was working bread dough. Patting heavier and firmer as he continued to heat her backside into a warm plane. The incredibly exciting tingle vibrated throughout her body, peaking her nipples and teasing the lubricant from her inner core. She sunk further into the mattress as she fell deeper into Walker's sensuality. She relaxed and absorbed the deliciousness of his work.

Before she realized it, cool, slippery liquid oozed between her buttocks, quickly warming as he rubbed it into her anus. That puckered entry point tightened at the implication of what he was doing. Her groan was elongated as he massaged her pulsing brown hole. He tapped that contracted muscle and spoke in a chastising voice.

"You need to relax, naughty girl, before I have to add a hard, bare bottom spanking to this punishment." Josie moaned as she fell deeper under his spell.

His finger pressed past the sphincter muscle and forged on roughly. He put more lube on the area. He twiddled her clit a few times while she tried hard to relax her backside. He pushed in two of his thick digits, scissoring on entry, causing her ass and core to flex and then clamp down on the intruders. Her moans were beginning to sound tortuous, but she couldn't help it. It was torment in the sweetest, naughtiest way. She shouldn't want him to continue, but she did.

LEANING DOWN TO KISS her luscious ass, Walker swatted her bottom with a little more snap. Her cry of half-surprise at the tingle, half-whimper of desire, was all he needed to hear to continue. Walker was always watchful when he edged or did anything more than the missionary position with his girl. Hurting her was the very last thing he wanted to do. To avoid even the mistake of rolling over her boundary line, which he knew changed according to the situation and her mood, he checked in with her.

"You okay, sweetheart? You hurt anywhere?"

"Only in a good way. Don't stop, please."

"Good enough." He leaned down to speak, his mouth close to her ear, his breath hot on her cheek, his voice, sensual and sexy. "I was going to finish the funishment part so we could get to the reward for being so good part, but I think I have the wrong end of the stick, eh darlin'?"

She released an impatient whine. Walker slapped her ass, his fingers grazing her slippery lips, then stopped to rub in the sting. Repeating that several times, testing her for readiness, he squeezed additional lubricant down her crack and fiddled with his toy before he withdrew his fingers. She huffed her dissatisfaction, and he tapped her pussy again.

"Patience, woman."

Her whimpers were so cute. She was trying to control the play with her sounds, knowing he would paddle her backside if she tried to ask for what she wanted with words. Now wasn't the time to do that. She knew exactly what she was doing, and so did he, but if it got her out of this nasty mood and moving forward, he wouldn't stop her. He liked being the advancer in the bedroom, but mutual play was fun too. But not today. Today was all about meeting the goal of release.

He pushed the heavy plug he'd been holding, nestled in his groin to keep warm, into her softened bottom hole. He knew the plug was measurably larger than his two fingers, but he knew how to make that work. Besides, this was not a new experience for his girl. She begged for this play and had forced him into this type of funishment many times.

In and out, he played with the toy and her back entrance. It had an impressively wide bottom and would bring on a sting when he ultimately pushed it past her sphincter muscle. It was the burn she loved to hate. In and out, and when he had primed her hole to accommodate all but the large bulbous base, Walker slid the plug to that widest spot and stopped right at the muscle. No advance, no retreat. The toy simply held the line, holding her entrance open, her muscles clenching and relaxing.

Her whine of sweet torture was exquisite. Josie knew not to move, leaving the ache and sting to be felt dramatically. If his girl's cries of desperate fulfillment were any indication, it was the perfect size toy for now. He twisted it and slid it slightly out, not filling her as she really wanted.

"No moving, baby or I will get the next size." He wiggled the nearly embedded plug, increasing her throbbing want. Walker played with her back entrance as he snaked his other hand to her clit.

"I'm going to play now."

"Isn't that what you were doing?" came her hoarsely panted reply.

"No, it isn't. I've been teaching you that if you trust me, I will make it good for you. Now time to come, baby."

After a few introductory flicks of her fattened clit, coated with the honey from her weeping core, he put his hand to her opening and could feel the inner muscles clutching for something to hold. He could help her out. There was the rhythmic clicking of the bracket rolling over the zipper teeth, unfastening his pants. He slid his jeans and underwear partially down.

Walker then used his pelvis to put pressure on the plug to hold it steady, not quite fully seated and only wiggling slightly. Slapping her bottom lightly again, he tweaked her clit as he shoved the plug completely in with his pelvis. Josie screeched. Walker pulled his finger away from her clit, grabbing her hips as he plunged deeply, his cock touching her womb in one hard, fast movement.

Josie grunted, moaned, and pushed her ass back into his pelvis in a countermovement to make his thrusts sink as deep as possible. He had been holding back while he edged Josie, so Walker soon felt the heat move down his spine in a tingling rush of blood that signaled his beginning orgasm. He reached around and located her clit with unerring accuracy, flicking and rubbing just to the side of her tip, knowing it was where experience told him she felt the most zing. Josie's movements became feverish.

He slapped the flank of her ass. "Stop moving. This is my game now."

She stopped immediately, but he knew it cost her to do so. If she had continued, they would have climaxed, but she would not have had as sparkling of a result as she always experienced when he demanded she not move. It forced her to feel the rush, the burn that comes from letting go and something else. His baby needed to learn to accept what came and allow the relinquishment of her control. It was a great way of teaching.

Like a freight train, his orgasm was building, charging forward fueled by the painfully powerful release that crashed over Josie. It appeared to ravage her as a monster wave on a rocky shore, violent and beautiful. Walker pulled out the plug a few inches and then plunged it in as he rammed his cock inside her. So... fucking... tight with both sexy entrances plugged. Her inner core muscles were rippling, and that extra sensation brought his orgasm to a final fiery explosion, flames licking over him, consuming him.

Slick with sweat and worried he had been too rough with her, Walker kissed her glistening back and neck, careful not to lay over her prone form, moving off Josie as soon as his body would comply with his brain's command to do so. He lay next to her, watching the woman he loved as she recovered from the hottest fuck they had had in weeks. Life had gotten in the way of them as a couple. He vowed he would try and make sure that it didn't happen often. As he lay there beside his lover, neither fully on the bed, regaining his peace and his breath, he made sure she was recovering as well.

Her skin glistened and glowed with a deep flush. Her eyes were closed, but she still sported a euphoric flavor to her slight smile. Walker reached his hand out to her.

"Baby? Ready to move up on the bed better? Let me hold you."

"Mmhmm." She made no movement. He waited a little longer.

He spoke again, his voice a little firmer. "Josie honey, you have to let me help you crawl up."

"Do I have to?"

Her voice still had a dreamy quality to it. Walker knew she would crash soon if he didn't get her up and cuddled in. He'd made sure she was sated, and he had to smile that she was so boneless. Mission accomplished. Some women he had been with hated any type of cuddle time, but his girl, while saying she didn't need it, craved it. Much more recovered now, he slid off the bed then half picked, half pulled her onto the spot he had prepared for her and went around to the other side to situate her better. She really had no intention of helping, and he was fine with that.

Josie had a moment of obvious tenderness on her shoulder as she tried to cuddle into his arms, but as soon as she found a comfortable spot, she settled in. Walker knew they would have to eat dinner sometime, but right now, holding his girl and lounging in the afterglow of their togetherness was more than enough sustenance.

Chapter 11

The next morning, Josie woke with a delicious ache, but she was in a much better mood than she'd been in since the accident. After taking an analgesic, she showered, then dressed in clothes that were easy to manipulate on and off. She'd created a section in her closet to house the right attire to lessen the time spent searching. It was slow progress because it was still painful when she moved her shoulder, but she expected to be cleared for office work and start her PT after the doctor visit today.

She felt as though she was about to get some of her life back, and that put a skip in her step. That, and the fact that Josie had decided to fight back by helping to uncover who attacked her. She expected that it was a prank; however, the Knight brothers needed to deal with it to regain order. Josie needed to find the culprit so she could take back control of her thoughts. A win-win in her book.

Josie got in her car and drove to the ranch office. Walking a mile to work never appealed to her. Walking home was a different story. Sometimes she did that, but Walker was always there to drive her back the next morning. She was ready to go a little early, a little out of character for her, so why not check-in to see if there was anything needed in town. This was Camille's day to work at the school, so Josie didn't bother asking her. As she topped the stairs and entered the office, she found it empty except for a ranch hand rummaging in her desk. She firmed her voice, channeling the men's chastising tone.

"Excuse me, who are you and what the hell are you doing in my desk?"

The man jumped nearly out of his skin, and it would have been comical if it wasn't so damn irritating and violating. She had her phone up and snapped a picture of the now anxious young man. Once she had her photo that automatically uploaded to her cloud storage, she called Walker. The call went to voicemail, indicating he was out of the coverage area. She dialed another number.

"Listen, the boss sent me up here to find the sale sheets."

"For what?"

"Um, how should I know? For whatever. He said they were on your desk."

"And then why are you inside my desk?"

"Couldn't find the sheets on it."

"Walker would never have sent you to look for sheets as he knows I store them on the computer. He has access. He would have printed it off, *at his desk,* if there were paper copies."

She held her hand up to stop his answer. "Sawyer," started Josie. As she began to rapidly fill in the other boss man, the young man in the office bolted. She walked to the window to see which direction he went and relayed that information to Sawyer. "I'm forwarding his photo to you and to Walker. Do you have a key to the office? Good, I have an appointment, but I'm going to lock it. You'll need your key to get in." She listened to Sawyer a few more seconds, his conversation degrading to mostly four-letter words, and then they hung up.

Getting into her car and heading off the Clear Knight, Josie was sure she saw the same young man go into the stable office. That was where Renfro had worked, the stables and that office. She stopped and sent a quick text off to the guys again before she headed into town.

The clinic appointment was not as exciting as Josie had hoped. "Light duty, and only half days." When she complained, Doc, who had known the Knight family for years, frowned in a strikingly familiar way. "You'll thank me soon. If you follow directions, young lady, you will be ready for full days, but still light duty when you come back. If not, well, you will be on half days for a lot longer." He waited to allow that to sink in before continuing. "Now, I have sent over what result I'm looking for in physical therapy, and the therapist will send me back the schedule for approval. I'll see you back here in two weeks." Josie sighed but nodded her understanding.

Physical therapy was just what it sounded like, a little painful, sometimes more than a little, repetitious, and it pushed her boundaries. The therapist said the best thing for her was to rest and ice her muscles, occasionally rotated with heat. Tired, but in a good way, Josie popped a couple more over-the-counter painkillers before stopping to grab a few groceries and items she needed. Satisfied, she started home. Her adrenaline was ebbing quickly, leaving her ready for a nap. Walker would be thrilled.

As Josie approached the ranch, all she could think about was getting back home and getting a little sleep. Suddenly, seemingly out of nowhere, a truck came barreling in her direction, on her side of the road. Josie screamed. Thinking she was about to have a head-on collision, she yanked the wheel. Gravel flew and hit her windshield, she ran over a milepost, and then a reflector post, before stopping on the grassy knoll beyond the shoulder. The truck continued down the road.

It took a few minutes for Josie to collect her thoughts. She was safe, and other than some damage to her vehicle, it was all good. She had survived. Her car was still on, and she called Walker, who answered on the first ring. "Hey, darlin'. How'd the appointment—"

"I was in an accident, Walker. Can you come get me?"

"Hell, baby, are you okay? Do we need to call an ambulance?"

"No, I'm not hurt, not really. My car, on the other hand..."

"Not worried about your car. We can replace that." Josie could hear Walker take a deep breath and exhale. It was his method of calming down. "Now, where are you, baby?"

"I can almost see the ranch from here. I was nearly home."

She could hear keys jingle and his boots on hardwood floors as he began to come get her. She heard Walker speak to someone in the room with him, and the next thing she heard was two sets of boots and a slamming door. Figuring she could turn the car off now, she disconnected her call when she shut off the ignition key.

As she sat waiting for the guys, it didn't take her much connective thought to conclude that all this happened because she had given up her control. She should have shut those men down right away when they had bothered her. Josie now wished she had shown them she was not a pushover and asserted what authority she had instead of playing nice. Sawyer had been right to advise her to show her strength early. Neither he nor Walker had any qualms about firing the worst of the offenders, and she had protested. Well, lesson learned.

It took the Knight brothers two minutes to find her and pull in behind the sadly banged up Kia Forte. She liked this car, she thought sullenly. Hadn't she dealt with enough lately? She'd never get what she paid for it from the insurance company to replace it, and she hated car payments. To top it off, she was tired and hungry and *sore*. She had been sore for one reason or another most of the last month.

The truck that had just run her off the road must have come from the ranch. This was the last straw. It was all she was going to take from the ranch hands. She had been right when she had declared to Walker that she couldn't trust anyone but Cody and the Knights, and she would get tougher. The party was over. She had no intention of allowing others to dictate whether she and Walker were a couple or if she worked on the ranch or anything else. Josie was plenty worked up by the time the two Knight men had arrived, having been pulled away from their chores, Walker was surprisingly gentle when he spoke to her.

"Be still, baby. Let us look at you first."

"I've already moved all my parts. They're sore. I'll probably hurt like the devil later, but nothing more than bumps and bruises."

The men spoke in varying degrees of anger and openly planning how to not only find the man but draw and quarter him. The words they used gave Josie a little giggle. *Possessive much?* Yeah, she was mad as hell at this being the culmination of a sucky month, but these boys right here, they were peeling the paint off her limping car. And it felt good to have someone take up for her. She grinned harder. She had called them for help without even thinking about it. Progress in the midst of chaos.

"You sure, baby? Maybe I should take you back to Doc, just to be safe. You might have done something you don't know about."

"Nope, I'm good. Achy from my ass up, but I'm fine."

That statement seemed to slow Walker down. Sawyer was on the phone, getting someone from the ranch to bring their winch truck. She knew they usually used it for things like broken tractors and other large equipment. Seemed hardly worth the effort for her little car.

"It's okay. I can call my insurance and have it towed to the shop in town." The men stopped talking. Josie looked up from her phone and saw them staring at her as though they were trying to understand what she said. "What? Don't they have a tow truck at the garage?"

Still obviously confused, Sawyer said, "Why are you calling a tow when we have one on the way." He waved in the direction of the ranch. "Here it is now. We'll decide what to do when we get it home."

Walker nodded towards his truck. "Hop in honey, it's warm inside."

"But I need to call and get this reported."

Walker stopped. "It was a one-car accident."

"Two-car, or rather truck and car. I was smaller."

"Wait, you didn't just hit the shoulder wrong?"

"Of course not. I'm a good driver."

"Hey, Sawyer, hold up." Walker turned back to Josie. "Someone *ran* you off the road?"

"Yes, that's what I said," she said with a frustrated shrill to her voice. Josie was too exasperated to speak in normal tones.

"No, you said you were in an accident. When there were no other vehicles, we naturally assumed..." He shrugged his shoulders.

"Well, that proves the adage about assumptions. I was nearly hit head-on, and the driver knew what he was doing."

"Who was it?"

"I don't know, I didn't get a chance to see. The truck was big." Walker looked over at her car. "I know what you're thinking, they all look big from my little car, but it was big and black."

"Bigger than any of our trucks?"

"Kinda like Jackson's, but different. I'm not sure how it was different, but it was."

He reached in and helped her out. "Get in the truck," said Walker, a little more distracted from Josie's words. With a new focus, he and Sawyer started a whole fresh round of colorful conversation.

"Call Randy. Looks like we are going to need him to write it up. Ask him if we can get the car home, at least." Officer Randy Cambridge was a family friend and a local deputy running for sheriff. The old one was retiring. He'd be a good one if he were elected.

"Right." Sawyer turned away from the wind to dial.

As Sawyer was making the call, Walker turned and seemed to realize Josie was still out in the cold with not enough on to keep her warm. "Why are you still out here? Let's get you in the truck, honey."

"I'm good. Honestly, I'm just trying to think what was different about this black truck."

"Josie, you can think while you're in the cab, and it will be warmer. Jeezes woman, where is your coat?"

"Home. I didn't expect to have this happen and it isn't really more than chilly. I'm tired. I'll just walk home."

"No, I'll run you. Sit tight a minute."

Josie wanted to tell him she could walk, and she could, but it was more than she wanted to do right now. If he drove her, it would be better. She was tired, achy, hungry, and getting sleepy again. She climbed into the cab of the truck and leaned to the side, glancing up at the rearview mirror. These Knight boys loved their pickup trucks, and they had every fancy doodad inside. That was it! Josie opened the door too fast and let out a screech.

In a flash, Walker was standing in front of her with Sawyer coming behind, still talking on the phone. "What happened? Did you fall?"

"I opened the door too fast, and it yanked my muscles." Big tears welled up, but she was determined not to let them fall. She wiped her good arm across her eyes and sniffed. "I know what was different." The men looked at her. She shook her head in exasperation. "About the trucks." Understanding shown in their faces. "Piper's garter."

"What honey?"

"Piper's garter, that is what Jackson has on his rearview mirror. Blue and white. In the truck today, red and white beads were swinging from the mirror."

Walker kissed her as Sawyer started talking faster. "Sawyer is going to make sure the sheriff's office understands. They're going to take care of that right now, and when he gets back, we're taking you home. Up you go. You need a nap, and I need to know you're safe, so you are sleeping in the main house on our bed."

"Walker, I need my bed."

"Baby, that is your bed. Are you sure you don't need Doc to check you over?"

"No, I mean my bed in my place."

"You'll get it, just not right now. I need to take care of you for the moment."

He put his hand up to end her arguing. Josie held her tongue. The few times Josie had seen Walker or any of his brothers take on this hard of a line, they meant business. She still remembered her time on the Gentry Ranch now Clearwater Gentry when she worked for Piper. When things got rough, these men went caveman. She could accept this 'take no prisoners' attitude right now. Besides, she was tired, and while it was normal for her to take charge of her own life, she couldn't deny it was nice not to have to do it. She sounded like Camille, and that made her smile.

"You aren't going to be alone in the cottage, and that isn't a request. Argue and complain all you want; it won't make a bit of difference except you might go to bed with a hot ass for your trouble. Josie, I'm taking care of you, and you will let me."

Walker talked big but while he might threaten, he just wanted her to let go. He had no intention of following through. Josie yawned. "I'm not arguing with you, Walker. I've hit my limit for today."

She saw when he softened. His jaw lost its hardness, his eyes lightened. Josie relaxed when Walker slid his hand over her thigh, wrapping his fingers around her inner softness. She nearly scooted closer so that his fingertips, so close to her apex, could brush her newly trimmed and more sensitive muff and delve into her pink bits, but he was distracted, and she was nearly asleep. Satisfaction would have to come later. She hoped they were in the mood later.

When the trio finally made it home, Belinda made clucking sounds as she fussed over Josie, and in an odd way, Josie wished this hadn't been Camille's day to work because she just needed some nurturing. She would never admit it openly, but this family and the way they took care of each other, was growing on her. And even though she acknowledged he was probably right, and it gave her more secure comfort, Josie was grumpy about her new restrictions. Boundaries that she wanted to object to and did until that liquid warmth flowed through her as Walker nearly begged her to do it his way for now.

She gave in and let him feed her soup for lunch and put her to bed. He kissed her tenderly, covered her and left her to rest. Snuggling deep into the down comforter, she couldn't remember when she had felt this protected in a long time. Her mother was nurturing, but she also came with so much baggage that Josie always felt she had to protect the younger children from the results of their mother's lifestyle. Here, she thought, she had finally found a place that accepted her for who she was. But was that enough when, based on today's and previous events, someone didn't want her here.

Josie admitted she loved Walker and was well on her way to being in love with him. While she was driving home, still recovering from her PT appointment, she had contemplated leaving but decided that was ridiculous. After Josie left her mother's trailer and the broken odds and ends Josie had as possessions that were typical during her childhood, she decided no one and nothing was going to push her out of where she wanted to be. She held her head up high and was proud of who she was. And she wanted to be here.

Yes, she had areas that needed improvement, but she was part of the human race, after all, riddled with imperfections some more adorable than others. No, she was going to stay and fight for what was hers and what she wanted. That is if she could even get those Knight boys to allow her any freedom to root out the problem and apply the solution. She would have to be as compliant as she could be, and with the release to light-duty and half days recommended, she would be able to go back to the office. Walker wouldn't see her as such an invalid, and she could work on figuring this whole mess out after she closed her eyes for a few minutes. She rolled over and went to sleep.

Chapter 12

Walker's brothers were as confused as he was. The sheriff had come and gone, electing to allow Josie to sleep before interviewing her. Walker had promised to bring her into the office the next day. That feeling of a bug racing up the back of his neck had happened several times recently, and he had ignored it, but now, with all this happening, he wasn't about to ignore any tingle or twitch that was out of place. Someone was out to hurt his baby girl, and that was not going to continue.

The Knights were worried. Camille had come home under escort, the children were not allowed to play without supervision, and while Lily was fine with it and Colton was too small anyway, Eli chafed at the constraints.

"Daddy, I want to go play in the hay barn."

"Sorry, son, but you need to stick close to home today."

"That is close. You can see it from here."

"Boy, it's a half-mile from here. I know it doesn't seem like far, but you'll have to go another day."

"But you can still see it from here."

"Not today, Eli."

Eli sounded like his mother as he grumbled, but a lift of Sawyer's eyebrow stopped him in his tracks, just like his mother.

Sawyer waited until Eli was out of earshot before he chuckled. "That boy is his mother's child."

Jackson's chortle brought a questioning look from Sawyer. "I thought he was a chip off the ol' block."

Sawyer nodded. "Yeah, you're probably right. Camille usually minds eventually, but she does insist on trying things her way first."

"That's what I'm afraid of," said Walker grimly.

"What?"

"Josie's cut from the same cloth as Camille, only she is worse. She is between Camille and Piper. She doesn't ask for help, she doesn't wait for assistance, and she doesn't always accept it when it's offered, even when she really needs it."

"I can see why you're worried. We have to have your girl buy-in if protecting her is going to work," said Jackson, who had come over when he heard about the incident. "Piper nearly... well, we all know how the shit can hit the fan without warning. You've got to talk to Josie and get her to see reason."

"I know," said Walker as he got up to pace again.

From the door of the den came a female voice. "I'm willing to work with you, but the operative word, gentlemen, is 'with.'"

"Hey, sweetheart. Feel better?"

Walker sighed in relief as his question was met with a smile. At least she was starting out receptive. He crossed the room and took her lips in a deep kiss, needing the reassurance that his woman was all right, even though he hadn't kept her safe thus far. He chose to ignore her statement for now and hoped she would let him totally disregard it because he had no intention of letting her do anything that might put her back in danger.

"Mmm, that was nice. Did we have dinner yet?" Josie smiled dreamily.

"Nope, be about twenty minutes. Come sit with us, and let's talk about what happened today."

Josie sighed dramatically but nodded and followed him to the sofa. "If I can get something to drink, I'll have no objections."

"Josie, baby, you had pain meds earlier..."

She put up her hand. "Relax, I'll do fine with water."

Sawyer strode to the bar and opened a cold bottle of sparkling water, threw a lemon slice in a glass and poured the water before handing her the glass. Josie smiled her appreciation before speaking with blatant resignation.

"Now, what do you want to know?"

"First, what happened today. When did you discover there was a problem?"

Walker was the brother who thought things out, and she had no doubt he had run every scenario he could already. She would simply be verifying which one he would look at harder.

"After I turned onto the county road that runs in front of the ranch, I topped the last hill before our ranch turn-in. Then the black truck came out of nowhere, but now that I think of it, he must have come out of our drive because there isn't another one before the next hill. He crossed the road in a way that made me think it was no accident. Nonetheless, I think I honked but he never moved out of my lane. When it was clear I couldn't get out of his way, I braked hard and yanked the wheel, taking out a few of those posts before ending up in the ditch. He continued past me."

Jackson asked, "Did he get into his own lane afterward?"

She crinkled her face as if to say, *do you not see how dumb that question is?* before leaning into Walker. "Nope, I was too busy trying not to throw up and praying my thanks for living through it."

Jackson didn't seem to take notice of her sarcasm. Josie grinned. Now she understood Piper when she said she could get away with murder when Jackson was in one of his deep contemplative moods.

Josie posed a question to the group. "Do you think that the man who was rifling through my desk might have been the one in the truck?"

"What?" asked Jackson. Sawyer filled him in.

"Seems a good likelihood. We a never found him but where could he have parked? And why didn't anyone notice him?" asked Jackson.

Walker answered. "The truck looked like yours so most, if not everyone, who saw it parked wherever would have figured it was you."

Sawyer whistled. "Damn. We need to figure this shit out."

"Daddy, that is a yucky word." Lily's little chastisement brought a smile to the adults' faces.

Sawyer shifted in his chair and sat straight with his arms out in invitation. Lily ran into them and he hoisted her onto his lap. "Well, Miss. Piccadilly Lily, why are you listening to daddy's conversation? And I'm sure your auntie and uncles don't mind a little yucky sometimes."

Lilly was serious as she shook her head resolutely. "No, mommy said no yucky words." She put out her open palm.

Sawyer sighed dramatically and pulled out a dollar placing it in her hand. "I wonder where you get being such a stickler for rules from?"

She hopped down and ran the curse jar. "Don't know. Mommy, I got another dollar!" she yelled as she ran from the room.

Lily brought a little chuckle from each of the adults before the room grew quiet again. Josie's mind shifted back to the cluster of events that could have easily caused her great harm. What is going on, and how could she find the truck, and thereby the owner? Then it dawned on her, track him down, or in her case, stake out the grocery store. Only one food market in town and everyone used it. She wasn't going to share her idea just yet. These men would veto the idea and it was a good one. She was protected here, she knew it was her refuge from her past and present but would be her fortress in the future. But she had to get there first.

Eli stuck his head in the door. "Dinner and Miss. Belinda says wash your hands if you've been back outside."

Jackson laughed as he snagged his hat. "Piper and I are going out so I'll have to take a raincheck on dinner."

The discussion turned to other things with the children at the table.

After waiting another whole week and no one finding the truck that had run her off the road, or the person who had put nettles under her mare's saddle still not identified, Josie had had enough. Enough waiting, enough sitting, enough taking it easy... just plain enough. Grabbing her bag and the keys to her car, she headed out. It was possible and even likely that the same man did both things, but why?

As she was locking the cottage door, a rough, demanding voice made her jump. "Just where the hell are you going?"

Dammit. Just the person she was trying to avoid. "Walker, you startled me."

"I'm going to do more than that if you're going to do what I think you are."

"Go to physical therapy? Why don't you want me to go?"

"Is that where you're going? I thought that was tomorrow."

"I get to try swimming today to build the muscles back up without too much pressure. Do you need me to stay?"

Walker cocked his head to the side and changed his tone. "No, baby, I'm just worried about you going anywhere alone. Who is going with you?"

"With me?" she squeaked. "No one." She inched toward the car.

"Josie, you know that isn't going to happen while we're still trying to find out who's behind all of this. I can't leave, but I'll send a hand with you as a precaution."

"Fine. If you can find one you trust besides Cody. I'll go to the house, and you can call him. I don't think it's necessary, though. I mean, it's been a week, and nothing has happened. I've worked in the office every day since the accident."

"You forget we haven't left you alone, honey. Please just let me do this for a while longer."

"I already said, okay."

He reached out to Josie and pulled her close. His hot breath, laced with coffee and mints, washed over her in a comforting way. His cologne, woodsy and spicy filled her nostrils, relaxing her tense muscles, and his entire essence gave her a sense of peace. That's what this man did for her. He completed her. How could she do something that would not only very likely get her spanked, but it would also erode their relationship? But how could they go on if they didn't resolve this?

Walker kissed her with a gentle hunger. She could hardly breathe from the intoxication of it. This rancher was the real deal. Not like those men she'd dated, nor like the men her mother went out with that seemed always to have been panting after her. Useless, looking for what they could get out of the pairing, not expecting much from the encounter except physical gratification.

Walker Knight could dominate a room when he entered it if that was his intention, or he could stand quietly and observe, which garnered him a different type of attention. Women loved his maturity and his singular attention to whomever he was speaking with. Josie had even noticed how he was able to be fully engaged in a deeper conversation but still show her he knew she was there by just a rub of her back, a squeeze of the hand he had on her waist, and if they were in a group of family or friends, he would kiss her temple or place his hand on the back of her neck. She freaking loved that.

Being the administrator of the Clear Knight Ranch and co-administrator of the Clearwater-Knight Enterprises, the eldest Knight brother was firm but fair, gentle but strict, and one hell of a lover and protector. Josie sighed. That was all he was trying to do, take care of her like he felt was his responsibility. And he wouldn't go back on his word that she could help him find the truck guy, but she knew all agreements would be void if she went against him.

"Walker."

"Yeah, baby?" He perused her face and damned if that man didn't already know she was about to do something she shouldn't. "Spit it out. I know something's up. You have that look like you've done something you shouldn't have."

"No, really, I didn't." He lifted his chin slightly. Josie rolled her eyes. "Honest. It's just that... well... I was going to."

He hiked his brow, his voice already chastising, "Go on."

"Well, I was going to go sit at the grocery store and wait on the truck. Maybe drive around town a bit, looking for it at noon, and maybe dinner time."

He nodded. "Go on."

"Well, I thought if I could find the truck, then we could let the sheriff know."

"It's not a great plan, but it is a good thought. Noon brings plenty of people to town for lunch. After work, more go to the grocery store, but baby, you can't sit out there that long. It's still cold enough to find you freezing, and it's a waste of time just sitting when you don't know when or if he'll come."

"Oh, he'll come. And the office is caught up except for all that old filing and digitizing the records. If I sit there and do that all day, I'll go mad. I can split it between trips."

"Okay, look, I need to go help Sawyer this afternoon, but you promise me you will file and scan and whatever you have to do, in the office, until four, and then we will take a drive through town. Right?"

"But he might come in at lunch."

"And he might not. The sheriff's department had been looking and so far, nothing."

"The sheriff's department is under new management, or soon to be. Didn't the older man retire?"

"I'm not allowing you off this ranch alone. Not right now. I appreciate you could have gone without telling me, but I'm more relieved you had a change of heart. You are the most important person in my world right now until we have children then you'll share that spot. I have to do better than I have thus far to keep you safe. I need you to trust my judgment, and for now, that is keeping you close."

"I fight my own battles, Walker. It's important to me that I do what I can and not ask for help."

"Honey, I do understand that and why, but you have to start trusting me and," he put his hand up to stop her response, "let me do what I can. I appreciate that you called me right away when you were run off the road. It means you trust me to have your back, and I understand how hard that is, which is why I offered to take you with me. If I thought you would go half-cocked and put yourself in the middle of a hot spot, I would never let you go. Don't make me regret my decision because it's already against my better judgment."

Knowing Walker was honest and didn't sugarcoat the truth, she had no doubts that if she rocked the boat, he would put his foot down and maybe even swing his meaty paddle-like hand down on her butt without remorse. Josie, on the other hand, would be regretting it plenty. She might not even get any sexy time. She huffed her annoyance as she looked up at the larger-than-life man that had taken her crazy world and set it right and nodded.

He dropped another kiss before stepping back from her. "That's my girl. Now, do you have a PT appointment later today, or was that subterfuge?"

"It's tomorrow."

"That's what I thought. Are you walking to the office or driving?"

"Guess I should walk since I don't have anywhere to go, even though I don't know if it isn't someone on this ranch that has it out for me."

"Good choice." He hugged her then patted her bottom playfully. "And we are buddying up as always, even through meals, so don't worry." He waved her on to head out in front of him. The look he gave her was as though he could easily eat her up. As she passed him, a swat smarted her butt.

"Hey," she groused.

"That was for trying to pull a fast one. We will address the lying tonight."

"Wait, they were the same incident, and it isn't one of the areas of concern."

"We can address it now, baby, but I'm still a little upset about it, so I might swing the belt a little harder than I'd want."

Her eyes widened. "Belt?"

He shrugged. "If we address it now, it's all I have to handle business with, but later, I might have cooled down completely, and decide just a little correction of your thinking is necessary."

"I'm going. See you later." Josie started to walk away, and then she turned back to yell, "Don't forget me at four."

He waved in answer, laughing as he turned around. Josie knew he had no intention of addressing anything. He was just worried. She passed four workers on her way to the office. Everyone seemed out in force these days. She wasn't sure she was happy about that or more on edge.

THE DAY HAD BEEN QUIET. Not one person came into the office with Walker and Sawyer off doing ranch business. She had scanned, electronically filed, and then paper filed forever. Josie was sure her fingers were going to fall off because her mind surely would shut down with the boring repetition of it all. She looked over at the considerably smaller pile of work left and felt a little pride at the accomplishment until she glanced at the clock, four-thirty. Walker was supposed to be back already. She called Camille and caught her just as she was sitting down with the kids.

"Sorry, forgot you worked today."

Josie could hear Camille's smile on the phone. She wished she could be that happy all the time. Or maybe a little more than she was, anyway. "No problem, what's up?"

"Is Sawyer back?"

"Not yet, but sometimes I don't see him until six. He said he and Walker had some cattle to check out on one of the back pastures. They put them out a week ago, I think. Sawyer said it was warm enough and something about Jackson's breeding herd. I think they were worried about the count and a mama cow and her heifer. Anyway, why do you ask?"

"Walker was supposed to be back at four, and besides, they left this morning. That's a long time. I think I'm going to call his cell."

"Good luck. The guys put a tower up, but there are still dead spots. Anyway, call if there's a problem."

"I will, but I'm sure you're right."

Hanging up, Josie called both men's cell phones and found them going immediately to a message that said the phone was unreachable. So, no service. With a little irritation, she called

Camille and told her she was going home. "If Walker shows up, tell him I'm at the cottage."

"Sure thing. Do you want to have dinner with us? We always have plenty."

"My shoulder is aching. I'm going to clean up and take a pain reliever, but thanks."

By the time Josie had gotten home, she wasn't sure which feeling was stronger, the annoyance at having to put off their trip to find the guy in the black truck or her worry about where the guys were. As it got later and the light faded, Josie was worried. The Knights knew the place like the back of their hand. She also knew they were great survivalists, but the unease was more than she could tolerate, and she called the stables.

"Any sign of Walker or Sawyer yet?"

"No ma'am. Haven't seen hide nor hair of them. Cody said if we hadn't seen them by seven, that we were to go looking for them."

"That's in a few minutes. I'm coming with you."

"Now, Miss Josie, I don't think Walker would be too happy if we took you out in the dark with everything that's been going on. In fact, I know he wouldn't. He'll hand me my ass, to be blunt. Let me call Jackson and Cody."

"Well, you let me worry about that, will you? I won't let him blame you for me pushing you to do it. Go right ahead and call Jackson and Cody, but I'm going out, with or without you."

"Yessum. I don't think that will make any difference when he starts gnawing on my butt, but I'll be here. You want me to saddle Crescent?"

"Yes, thank you. Walker will be glad for the help if something has happened to them, and I'll be sure to credit you. I'll be there in ten minutes." She hung up and quickly grabbed her gear.

Chapter 13

Walker heard a moan off to the left, and he wondered who it was and where the hell he was. The side of his head hurt like a son-of-a-gun. Gun. Did he hear gunshots before he blacked out? It didn't seem like a good idea to try to sit up fast, so he lay in place and took stock of his surroundings. Yep, he was on the ground. Grass that had been grazed short, dirt, hard and cold lay beneath him. What else, Knight, listen. Another moan. It sounds like a kid. He tried to think, did he bring a kid out with him? No, just Sawyer and himself.

Sawyer, where was he? No one seemed to be moving around in the half-light, and as Walker's eyes focused on the surroundings, he saw two lumps of what was probably humanity stretched out on the ground. Things began to come back to him. They were on their way back after spending the morning separating some cows with another brand out of their herd, putting them in a different pasture to find out who they belonged to.

After lunch, they spent the afternoon trying to locate their cow and her heifer. The calf was in the ditch, and a distraught mama was standing watch and occasionally bawling. The two had wandered quite a piece off from the herd, and it was hard to find them until mama began to call to her baby again. The bawling drew them to the site. After the rescue, they made sure the infant could feed, and then mama and baby went back to the fold. Much longer, and they would have had a feverish mama and a weak baby.

Glad to have accomplished what they needed, the brothers started home, joking and talking. That's when they heard the report of the rifle. Walker heard the whiz of the bullet through the air just before he was knocked off his horse, then intense pain then nothing until now. What happened to...

"Sawyer. Sawyer, where are you?" No answer. Nothing but another moan that didn't sound at all like his brother.

Rolling to his belly, he crouched and then pulled his knees under him as he waited for his vertigo to settle. His stomach roiled. Damn, likely a concussion. He needed help. Not moving more than necessary, he reached back and pulled his phone from its holder on his belt. He checked for a signal. Damn, they weren't close enough to the tower. After taking a few slow, deep breaths, things righted themselves physically, and he slowly stood.

He whistled at great expense to his head. No response. Their mounts must have been spooked and went home. No matter how well trained a horse you had, they all had a limit to what they would put up with before high tailing it home. Well, showing up at the stables without their riders would get the message across that help was needed. He crawled over to the moan and found it to be Corey. The kid he'd had words with about bothering Josie a few weeks ago. The kid's shoulder looked shot. Damn, who could have done that? And why was he here?

"Hold on, kid," rasped out Walker. The kid made a noise in response, but he seemed well enough to stay where he was for now without any further assistance.

Looking around him, Walker saw the second lump on the ground. Sawyer? With slow, deliberate breaths fueled by his determination, Walker gritted his teeth and clenched his jaw. Getting to Sawyer was his main goal.

"Sawyer," he called the loudest he could.

He was angry. He couldn't get louder, not with his head pounding. It was all he was able to do. Finally, after what seemed like forever, he crawled up to his brother. Sawyer was still warm, Walker could hear his deep, easy breaths, and he almost cried his relief. *Okay*, he told himself, *see what's wrong with him.* It was easier said than done in the darkening light.

"Walker?" came the whisper.

"Yeah, Sawyer, I'm here. I'm right beside you. Where are you hurt?"

"My gut. I think a bullet got me in the side. I thought you were dead."

"Nah, can't kill me that easily. Who did this?"

"It looked like Corey, but whoever it was, I got off a shot and thought I winged him. At least I hoped I did."

Walker answered him grimly. "You did, and it was Corey. What the hell?"

Sawyer's voice became stronger. "No idea, but I do know that this is just about enough. I'm done with this shit, and we are going to handle business, law or no law. Where are the girls and the children?"

"At home, I imagine. I pray, anyway."

"God, I hope they're all right. We have to get to them."

JACKSON PULLED UP AND got out of the truck, slamming the door as he walked away from it. "You got me a horse?"

"Yessir. But I'm getting a little worried about everything. Your brothers' horses came back, and another of the workhorses, but without their riders. And I expected Miss Josie here by now, but she hasn't shown up. She was the one who called the alarm. Said she was sure something was wrong." Josh, the stable manager, indicated the horses, "Guess she was right.

"Okay, I think I'd better take the truck in case we need to haul someone injured back or haul ass to the emergency room. Grab some saddle blankets. Mount up with a couple of others and follow me." He dialed Piper. "Get over here and bring the baby and a few hands for protection. It might be a long night."

Jackson filled Piper in on what was going on as he walked to the truck. Then he called Josie. It went to voicemail. Damn. He stopped by the cabin and pounded on the door. No answer. He walked around and was surprised to see that the bedroom light was on. It looked like she had been getting dressed, but her riding boots were still by the bedroom door. A chill ran up his back, and he went all around the cabin. On the side of the cabin was her little car, still broken from the accident, and lying on the ground next to it was Josie.

"Cody, get to the ranch, all hell has broken loose. We need every hand mounted and carrying. Call an ambulance and the sheriff's office. Hurry, man."

"I'm nearly there. I got a call earlier. Getting off now."

Jackson called Jason Kirkland, his new ranch manager since their last one had tried to kill Piper. "I need the hands-on alert and you over here at the Clear Knight. Cody is going to need some help. We've had at least one attack, likely more."

"Right, boss. Give me a few minutes to get things going here, and then I'll be there. Where do you want me?"

"I've talked to Cody. He'll get you a search party. And follow Piper and Janine over, will you?"

"You got it, boss."

Jackson knew the managers would handle a search party and the rest of the ranch. His heart was torn. Stay with Josie and wait on the ambulance or find out where his brothers were. The question was answered when Josh rounded the corner and whistled.

"Is she..."

"No, but she has a knot on her head that worries me. She isn't bleeding much, and she is breathing easy, so stay here and let me go out through the fields. Cody is on his way, and he'll take care of things. Call him and update him. The ambulance should come here for Josie but tell them we may have two more that need services. Then get Camille out here to check on her but keep them protected. I want two men, three if we can spare them, in the house with the children and Piper. I want three out here with Camille and Josie, one with each of them at all times, understood?"

"Yessir."

"You armed?"

"Yessir."

"Good. I need two or three more guys out behind me with floodlights. I'll turn on my clearance lights. Hopefully, we'll be back soon. The sheriff should be on his way. Fill them in."

"I got it covered."

"Good man." Jackson wasn't about to lose his brothers if they were still alive to save. And if they weren't, heaven's angels wouldn't be able to save the men or women who did this.

WITH THE BROTHERS SUPPORTING each other, they made their way, stumbling and swearing to where Corey lay, mercifully passed out again. Sawyer lay down close by, and Walker sat between the two men, keeping watch. They faced south, the direction of the main house, and Walker unclipped his flashlight from his belt. It was too dark now to attempt to walk in, but he was sure the ranch would be out in force soon to find them. Walker needed to make sure no one rode over them. He grabbed Sawyer's light too.

Walker didn't know how long they'd been there, but he thought he saw what looked like headlights ahead. No, they were too high. Maybe his head was playing tricks on him. It hurt like a son-of-a-bitch.

"That someone coming?"

"Yeah, Sawyer, now that you confirmed it wasn't my scrambled brain, I think someone is coming."

Each taking a flashlight, they made a cross on the grass in front of them and then shone it over their bodies and then the ground in front of them and held it there. The light hurt his eyes, and Walker stared at the ground behind the torches' illumination. The truck stopped.

"Walker, Sawyer, that you?"

Sawyer answered so Walker didn't have to yell. "You took your sweet time, Jackass. Me and Walker and Corey have been here a long time."

"Hell, you didn't invite me to the party."

"No cell phone service."

"Shit, we need to fix that." Jackson grabbed onto his brothers and helped them up before hugging them for a minute. The trash talk was so he didn't cry. "What the hell happened to you three?"

Walker spoke. "I think young Corey shot us."

"The hell you say," said Jackson.

"Yeah, think we can go over this after I get checked out? I think I lost a little blood, and Walker's head isn't up to much standing. I think I winged the kid. Odd he isn't staying awake, though. He might have hit his head."

GETTING WALKER TO CLIMB in the ambulance was difficult. Jackson knew he'd be looking for Josie, and he didn't want to tell his brother right off how he'd found her, but it was the only way to get him past the double panel doors. The devastation on his brother's face was almost more than Jackson could bear to see. Piper would stay with the kids along with Belinda, and he and Camille would follow the rest to the hospital. Cody was staying the night, and Jason went home to handle the Clearwater tomorrow. Everyone else was on watch.

What a mess. What was going on, and why? Only after everyone was treated and had gotten some sleep, would they be able to even begin to piece this story together. Jackson had no idea how Josie was, and he didn't even want to think about what would happen if she was badly hurt. Her pulse and respiration had been steady and strong, but that knock on her head was worrisome. He spent the ride behind the ambulance talking to Camille. Their family had known Camille since she was a kid of twelve coming to a riding party at the ranch. Sawyer had been taken with her, and he never looked seriously at another woman again. Although the couple had their trials and hardships, they, like Jackson and Piper, were solid and growing stronger.

"Do you think Josie will stay after this?"

Jackson was pulled from his inner thoughts. "You think she might not? I thought she and Walker were, you know, permanent."

"I thought so too, but her history with Walker and the ranches might repeat. Especially since they aren't formally committed or anything. You have to admit, they have had a rocky relationship. Now, with all this happening to them," Camille shook her head and sighed, "I just don't know."

After a pause, Jackson said, "You'd like her to be your sister-in-law, right?"

"Yes, but what we want doesn't matter. The question is if Josie loves Walker enough to power through the debris and let Walker get to the bottom of this."

"We are all going to get to the bottom of this."

"I know, and she will too, but it only matters if Walker does it. I saw her before she was loaded onto the ambulance. She has a concussion, at least as bad as Walker's, I'd say worse, so there again she is not able to do her own solving of her problems. For Josie, that is big. She doesn't ask and doesn't easily accept help because her mother was too eager to ask and receive."

"I heard something about that. Walker is more closed mouthed than you women."

"Well, it's her story to tell, and Piper and I are good listeners. Turn into the after-hours parking lot. It's so much closer."

"We don't come here often, but it seems that once we do, we come in a cluster."

"I hope that isn't going to continue. I have all I can handle for a while."

"We all do, hon, we all do. Let's get in and take care of our family."

Walker was fit to be tied by the time Camille and Jackson walked into the hospital emergency department.

"What do you mean she is in a room? Which room? If you want to check me out, it will have to be with Josie close enough for me to see that she's all right."

Jackson was a brawny man and knew he'd need all he had left in him to get Walker under control. Camille diverted her attention to her husband and left Jackson with a smile of amused encouragement.

"Of course, I have a headache. I fell off my damn horse after that kid shot me. If his aim had been better, I could be dead. Now, where is Josie?"

"Hey, old man, settle down. I'll get her room number, and you let them check you out. I'll find out how she is. Just quit giving these pretty nurses any trouble."

It looked as though Walker was going to continue his tirade, but then he abruptly nodded and sat back on the treatment bed. Jackson waived the nurse back in.

"I'd be quick if I were you. Walker's woman is upstairs in a bed, and he hasn't seen her yet. I wouldn't put much store in him staying calm for long."

As the treatment team moved in quickly, Jackson smiled. Now to get the next carrot. He stopped in the room to check on Sawyer, who was lying calmly on the bed while Nurse Camille saw to his comfort and discussed things in depth with the doctor. She stopped and gave Jackson the thumbs up. Relieved, he continued to the admissions desk and got Josie's room number.

Walking back past the treatment room Walker was in, he hesitated, but decided to lay his eyes on Josie and make sure himself that she was well, and then tell Walker. That was all the time he could give the medical staff before he would need to tell a distraught Walker how his lady was doing.

Jackson headed for Josie's room. With his final carrot to dangle in front of Walker to behave and do what was required so he could be discharged and go to Josie, Jackson stepped into a darkened patient's room. If it weren't for a little light to the back of the bed, he wouldn't have known if he was in the right room or not.

Josie lay huddled in the bed, and her sniffles broke his heart.

"Hey, sweetheart. Why the tears?"

The tears slowed. With a shaky but hopeful voice, Josie asked, "Jackson? Is that you?"

"Yes, honey, it's me, and before you get worried, Walker and Sawyer are okay. They are just downstairs getting the once over before getting released."

"What happened to them?"

"I'll let Walker talk to you about it all, but they walked away with nothing more than some scrapes, a hole in Sawyer's side, and Walker has what looks like a mild-to-moderate concussion and a bullet burn on his arm. Guess he hit a rock or something when he went down. Don't stress, he is cussing a blue streak and clamoring to get to you, so he's going to be fine. When they release him, he'll be up here with you. I had to do some fancy footwork to get him to let them work on him. He is beside himself with worry over you."

She let out a little groan. "I'm okay. I have a concussion too. I guess not as light as Walker's, or they would have let me go home. My head CT looks fine, but they said the knot on my noggin is good sized. It's tender for sure, and I have to say that the room sometimes dances when I move, and they gave me something so that I won't puke. But the headache is the worst."

"Have they given you anything for it?"

Josie started to shake her head and hissed. "No, I guess it's not recommended, but I can take small amounts tomorrow. Ice for my head and not moving or using my cell other than to call, no computer or any screens, and no working for at least a week. Poor Walker hired me to do a job I've spent half of the time recovering from. Mostly I can't do much because the doctor said they wanted to watch me and give me another scan before they let me go home tomorrow, maybe. I'm sleepy, and I can sleep if I want, but they are going to come in every few hours tonight to make sure I am waking up. Someone said something about some wires but so far, I've been left alone.

"Do you want me to sit with you until you go to sleep? By the time you wake up, Walker will be in here."

Jackson watched her entire body relax and then stiffen again. "I don't want to put you out. I'll be fine."

"Josie, you are going to have to accept help, sweetheart. You're family and the Knights take care of their own. I'll tell

Walker to paddle that stubborn hide if you don't allow us to help you. I'll get some of your things moved back into the bedroom at the house. With Walker down for a few days, too, I think it's the best and easiest for everyone. Sawyer's not feeling too hot either, although he didn't hit his head."

Josie gave a pained smile at Jackson's attempt at levity. "I'm pretty sure that paddling is out for a while, but okay. I don't want to put anyone out, but I've learned you Knight men are not easy to dissuade when you've decided on things."

Jackson grinned broadly. "I was hoping you'd feel that way. I'm going to call Walker and see if he is available to talk to you... for a minute only." Jackson gave her a stern look.

"Okay," said Josie with a yawn.

"Walker. I've got someone here that can speak with you for just a minute. Hold on."

Josie took the offered cell phone. "Walker?" Her tears fell, and her voice quivered. She nodded, hissed at the pain, and then said, "Yes, I'm fine. Really. How are you?" She chuckled. "I don't believe you. I'm good here tonight so you go home when you can, and I'll see you tomorrow. I'll get a cab or something."

Jackson shook his head when he heard her because he knew his brother was not going to have any of that. He'd drive himself in to pick her up if Jackson would let him. That is if he could get him to leave at all.

"Okay, say good night, sweetheart."

Her big watery brown eyes nearly did him in, but Jackson knew how to take care of their women. Josie was his priority right now when his brother wasn't available. Walker spoke to his eldest sibling quickly, reassuring him that she was just too tired to do more than sleep, and hung up. Yeah, that man wouldn't go home at all. Jackson would see about another blanket for him and a pillow. That lounge chair would have to do. "Now turn over and go to sleep, sweetheart. I'll sit here until you do, and then Walker will be up here soon."

He sat next to her and rubbed her back until she fell asleep a few moments later, just as he did with his small daughter. He stopped at the desk and talked to Josie's night nurse. Feeling he had done what he could, he headed back down to the rest of the family.

Evidently, Corey had been sent to surgery, but since Sawyer was sure he'd only winged him, Jackson wasn't going to waste any of his energy on him tonight. He was a kid, so that was in his favor, and he was an employee, well up until today he was, but that was not enough to garner any sympathy from Jackson. After Jackson had learned earlier that Corey had been confrontational and sexually harassing in his manner and conversation to Josie, he didn't have any time for the boy. Not today. But that day would come and so would the penance for messing with the Knights.

Walker was talking to Randy Cambridge, the newly elected sheriff, when Jackson arrived. Once Walker was done with the interview, he headed straight to his girl's room. The hospital offered to put another bed in the room and Walker agreed. Soon, Sawyer had done his own talking to Randy, and he was ready to head home, too, even though they wanted him to stay. With Camille being a nurse, they reluctantly let him go. Jackson called Walker, who promised to let Jackson know when Josie was released. The remaining trio went home.

It had been a long night, and Jackson was glad to settle into the bed with Piper when he reached the ranch. They had two-thirds of their family home. They just needed the last couple, and the ranch could start to heal. Jackson knew there was going to be hell to pay for what had happened here tonight, but that was for another time. A day of reckoning was soon to come, but not today.

Chapter 14

Josie sat in front of the main house and kicked her feet on the porch swing. It felt like she hadn't worked in months while mentally and physically recovering from the Renfro assault to healing from the shoulder accident colliding into the concussion incident. Not to mention the car accident. In reality, it had only been a total of two months, but that knowledge didn't make her feel any better. She'd never been so prone to mishaps, except this was much more than that. This was contrived, and damn if it didn't feel good that she was surrounded by people who took it in stride to take care of her and work at stopping it from happening again.

It also grated on her life mantra of never allowing anyone to do for her when she could do for herself. She often did without if she couldn't do it herself. *Don't lean on them*, her inner survival voice screamed; her quieter, longing voice loved the support, craved it. She couldn't figure out why someone wanted her hurt or for her to leave the ranch so badly that they did these things to her.

Corey seemed like a decent, if misguided, young man, so why would he shoot at the Knights and try to get rid of her? That bothered her because the sheriff that interviewed her was quick to blame her incident on Corey, but that was wrong. Corey was already shot. And where was the gun? And Renfro, what had she done to him and was he somehow still part of this? Did he make bail? She thought not. No, it made no sense at all.

Hot tears of devastation rolled down Josie's cheek as she tried to school her thoughts to the realization that she would have to leave this ranch that she'd grown comfortable with and leave Walker, with whom she had fallen in love. She knew she couldn't stay and risk anyone else's life, including her own. Piper and Camille's precious children would be at risk as long as Josie stayed on the ranch. Josie took a moment to mourn the children she wanted so badly with Walker. That would never happen now. She couldn't imagine loving anyone the way she loved him.

The doctor had taken a week to release her to drive and to go back to a part-day work schedule, but no computers for another week, which meant it was time to go. She had worked for the rest of the week to see if she was indeed ready. She had lasted the morning, but if she could do a morning, she could do a whole day if she were pressed. Therefore, if she could work, she could leave and start again. She needed to go before she lost her nerve.

Just as she was about to rise and pack her things, she felt a large, calloused hand settle hot and firm on her neck, awakening her nerve endings in remembrance of a masterful touch, Walker. His timing was always the best and the worst.

After kneading her tensed neck muscles for a moment, he kissed the top of her head. Josie melted into a puddle of heated butter. It was more tenderness than she could handle right now, and her swift intake of air followed by her waterfall of misery drew a distressed response from Walker.

"Honey, what's all this about? Are you not feeling well? Did you come back too soon?" Josie could only shake her head in disagreement and begin to cry in earnest.

Walker shifted, and she felt when he sat and enclosed her in his muscled body. Instant warmth surrounded her amidst the scent of soap, outdoors, and sweat by a man doing an honest day's work. How she loved that scent. With no other thoughts but to be with him, Josie leaned into his welcoming arms and cried for the losses in her life.

The love Josie's mother had for her offspring was real, but the embarrassment she had subjected her children to had tainted that love. Josie endured the ridicule as she grew up knowing her siblings all had different fathers, and all the other injustices a bohemian-souled woman visited, unknowingly, on her children. The reality of her home life that forced Josie from home as early as possible still hung around her neck like an albatross.

Josie mourned her lack of finding a real connection in a world of entitled college students when she did leave home. A connection that she was unable to understand enough to forge. Then the consequences of clickish work environments that she didn't want to participate in because end results were more important to her than togetherness. Even though employers wanted her to do both. Her neighbors, who were comfortable in their own skins, highlighted the fact that she wasn't, making it impossible to settle easily in any location. Therefore, she did what she had to do to survive. She pushed everyone away, no matter how much it hurt.

The first time she had felt like an integral part of the group was several years ago when she was working with Piper and the Knight men at what was now part of the Clearwater–Knight ranches. Unfortunately, the drama at the time was more than Josie could handle. She had become too dependent on Walker, had begun to fall in love with him, and it was too early. It'd been too soon since she left her mother's world and the college experience of being an outcast to believe Walker when he promised things would get better. She wished she had listened and taken that scary step then. Maybe this mess would not be happening now.

Leaving Clear Knight, leaving Walker and his family, was the hardest thing she'd ever had to do then. Now, the loss of the one person in the only place that she had ever felt she could be a part of forever, a place that bound her as much as she was entwining herself to it, was overwhelming in its torment. Another torrential round of sobs followed the first, and soon, it was difficult to breathe. Then the slow, gentle swaying began.

"That's it, let it all out, baby, I've got you."

This rough and tumble cowboy, who administered two huge ranches, who was about to purchase a third, and was the head of an ever-growing family and its empire, was murmuring sweet nothings to her as she cried her heart out. Josie had thought she loved Walker, but this proved she loved him more than she could fathom. Josie imagined it would only grow with time, and that had her clawing to get away from this man. Physically and emotionally. She had to leave now, before...

Walker grabbed her hands and strengthened his voice. "Hey, now, I think it's time to settle down and tell me what's going on here. I love you, no surprise there, and whether you're ready to admit it or not, you love me. That gives me rights others don't have with you, such as holding tight while you cry and then finding out what caused you to cry in the first place so I can figure out if I need to protect your honor for what someone else did or spank your ass for something you did. So, time to talk, baby."

Josie had stopped crying and pulled up her proverbial big girl panties. She made a grand effort to sniff away her last tears. "Okay, if you must know, I have to leave."

"Leave what, the ranch? Leave me? That kind of conversation will definitely earn you a hot seat. Now, start explaining," he put his hands up as if to stop her words, "From the beginning."

Josie started to stand up and found she was held in place by Walker. "Walker." She allowed her troubled feelings to be heard.

"No, ma'am," he said sternly, "you stay right here and tell me, while you are in my arms, why you think you have to leave me."

"You can find anyone to do the job you hired me to do. I've been a waste of space because I haven't been able to do that job for several weeks."

"And?"

"Walker, someone wants me gone, and you and Sawyer were hurt because of it. I can't risk the children or Piper and Camille."

"They're safe, don't you worry about that. What else?"

Josie shook her head. "You're wrong. I like you, and I might even love you some, but I'm not in love with you."

"Now that is a lie, and you know how I feel about lying. We'll deal with that later. Right now, I'm still waiting on that good reason you say you have for leaving."

"Walker, listen to me. The next time one of you could be killed! That is more than enough reason to leave. It'll take you all out of harm's way. I can't have any more on my conscience."

"Why do you care? You want to leave the ranch, leave the family, leave me. It doesn't sound typical for someone who wants to go on their way, unencumbered, to also worry about whether they might be the cause of future trouble. It sounds like a woman who loves those people. It sounds like a woman who has a false sense of duty."

"Of course, I care. I love... um... like you. I don't want anything to happen to any of you, and so I need to go. Today."

"It couldn't be that you're afraid of your feelings for me, is it? Or that you're getting too attached to the ranch, the family, this way of life? I'd thought running away from the problem was not something you'd do again. Obviously, I was mistaken. You're trying to escape, just like you ran from connecting on your jobs, ran from your family home, and are trying to separate yourself from us here. You don't have to deal with your emotions, your attachments, or life in general if you go. You're telling yourself it's for our good, but it's a coward's way to live, and it stops now."

Josie sat up quickly, standing and pacing on the broad front porch. "That's unfair. I don't let things get in my way. I plow past them. When I'm given an impossible task, I do it. When someone pushes, I push back, and I do it all myself. I don't rely on others to handle any of my problems because they are *my* problems. This is my problem. We don't know why or who is doing all of this, but I am obviously the target. Therefore, the best thing for me to do is leave. That is me fixing the problem."

"And do what?"

"Start over. But at least I'll take the trouble away. Either it disappears, or it follows me, but I can handle that."

"Then let's figure this out together. Don't run, fight. Randy Cambridge called and said that Corey isn't talking, but things aren't adding up."

Josie couldn't stop herself from being diverted from her end goal. "It was nearly seven and getting dark by the time we decided to go after you. I was hit just after that. You and Sawyer were already shot."

"Then I don't see it. The story was that Corey came after Sawyer and me *after* he had rung your bell. No, something else is going on. You need to stop feeling sorry for yourself. You don't make a good martyr, sweetheart. Rather than standing apart, join with us, and stand up for what we all want, our way of life, our family, us."

"But you have no idea why Corey and Renfro did what they did, and we don't know where to start. And if Corey didn't hit me, then who did?"

"And if he didn't shoot us, then who did?"

"Right." She said enthusiastically.

"So, we figure it out and face it down. This is life, Josie. Sometimes it gives us peppers, and when they get too spicy, we roast them and add tomatoes to make salsa."

She turned from her pacing and stared at him for a few seconds before she started laughing. "Peppers? Salsa? Um, I think you mean, lemons and lemonade."

He grinned. "Nope, we're in Texas. We make salsa. And we spank our women if they lie to us and hide from their feelings. Then we love them forever, defend them and our families with all that we have. Together."

"But I'm not your family, and when I leave, I won't be your woman."

She stifled a sob with the last word, but it was audible. Her heart hurt thinking the words, saying them was devastating, but if she didn't lay things out right now, she never would. It was harder than leaving her siblings and her mother behind, knowing she wouldn't be back to stay.

"Now I'm beginning to see the problem. You think that you aren't part of this family already. Honey, you're a Knight even though I haven't put a ring on your finger yet. I'll rectify that soon, I promise. But we Knights take care of our family, we face the good, the bad, and the naughty together. I think we have a little of all that right here." He gave her a chastising look. "It's time you do what your heart is telling you is right. The decision is yours. Are you going to stand with us and take care of business, or are you going to sit on your hands in the backroom and wait for the rest of us to handle it? Because rest assured, you are staying here with us, with me, forever."

"I always fight my own battles."

"Then fight this one with us because we always do it together."

Walker wasn't going to make this any simpler than he already had. She knew that. He wasn't letting her go, and for some odd reason, that made staying easier. Josie had no choice; although she knew that wasn't actually true, her stubborn pride demanded she deal with it that way, for now.

"Fine."

"I'm going to have to work on that stubborn streak you have, little girl, but for now, I'm glad you agree. I don't want to hear that kind of talk again. This is your home, and we are your family. Now come in for supper, and we'll show you what it looks like when the Knights fight for what is theirs."

Josie moved toward the door but stopped as she tried to figure out how she lost this battle, already having the niggling of second thoughts invading her mind. The loud explosive sound of contact, audible even on the wide openness of the porch, of a hard hand as it landed on her rear immediately drew her hands over her insulted bottom. It wasn't pain she felt, but her mind was startled by the loudness of the sound. She looked up into his warning face, chin tucked, eyebrows raised high. "What the..."

"Watch that mouth, little girl. I've decided I'm adding foul language to the list of penalty behaviors. You're already in hot water. I was just giving you a reminder that I didn't forget what you've earned here. I'm in the mood to add to your comeuppance if you've got a mind to push me."

"Walker, I was upset."

"Are you saying you wouldn't have lied to me or hidden your feelings if you weren't upset about the Corey business *before* trying to convince me that you should leave me? That it wasn't a lie when you said you weren't connected emotionally to me, that you didn't love me, us? Because I know for an absolute fact that you *do* love me and are *in* love with me too, and it isn't news to anyone." That tone, it got her every time.

"Of course... I mean... um." Her shoulders drooped. "Never mind."

He nodded with resolve. "That's what I thought. Now let's go inside before your lover finds more to add to your naughty list tonight."

Josie, walking in front of Walker, rolled her eyes as she smiled. He loved her.

Dinner conversation was animated. "Josie and I are going over to Martin Acres tomorrow morning. I have a last appointment with old Martin's son. I think the price of the land is so good, I'll take the livestock as well." Walker took another bite of roast beef.

Sawyer leaned back in his chair. "He really has what I'd call a farm with too much acreage for someone without crops, but since Piper is stepping back from some of the administration now that Josie is here, I'd like to give the kids something to learn to work with. He has some pigs, which are money-making and fun for kids, and some chickens that I thought to bring over here for eggs."

Jackson nodded. "Want to bring over the geese and ducks too?"

"Could. Actually, let me get the inventory from Martin today and see what we really want from over there."

Piper spoke up. "How's the house and outbuildings?"

Walker put down his fork. "Good, actually. I hired an inspector, and he is going over the house tomorrow morning while we are walking the outbuildings and talking livestock."

"What are you planning on doing over there?" asked Camille.

Josie answered. "We've looked at the profit margin and think that the place is really set up to run cattle. Not breeding like Jackson, or equine like Sawyer, although we can accommodate over there with whatever is needed, but just running cattle. I asked for buffalo, and Walker said I could try a few so long as they don't come in contact with the cattle. Something about disease and aborting calves. I'm excited."

Piper asked. "So, instead of building a house, do you two think staying over on the Martin place might be a possibility? We're going to need to have a solid presence over there, and our foremen have their hands full. We need one just for the new place. It'd be a good start to train a solid worker to take it on."

"Actually, Josie and I have talked about it. What about cutting a back road to meet the two properties like we did between Piper's and ours when we joined them, and we'll administer from the new place. If the house doesn't need too much work."

Camille added. "You should be good unless it's been empty for too long. It has tons of space for a family and lots of bedrooms. It even has two family rooms. I'd love that."

"A couple of years, I think. Anyway, that will be the plan unless things change."

Josie said, "And what about the trouble with Corey and Renfro?"

Walker continued. "For now, both are dealing with the sheriff, and we are just going to be more careful. I think Renfro is still in jail and not sure why unless he couldn't make bail. But it does remind me that no one goes anywhere alone, and the hands already work the ranch with a firearm in case they run into trouble. Usually, that's with wildlife, but these days, who knows. We'll just step it up to near the house and stables, too."

Josie answered. "I can't put everyone out for my problem."

Jackson looked at Walker. "I thought you were going to take care of this." He turned to Josie. "Josie, if I read things right about Walker's intent for the last few years, you're family.

The Knights take care of family, so that means you. I told you that in the hospital."

"It isn't fair to all of you."

"Why, because of the ruckus it has caused?" asked Sawyer. "Have you stopped to think that we might consider it our fault that you've had to deal with it on our ranch with our people?"

"You didn't do it. It's not your fault," said Josie.

Walker spoke up. "Agreed, just as none of it is yours."

"Oh, I guess that's true."

Walker leaned over and kissed her lips. "Yes, oh."

Walker didn't let her wiggle out of the situation by keeping their earlier discussion quiet.

"Josie thought she would save us the time and energy of figuring this all out by taking off in the hopes of dragging the trouble along with her. Or maybe she hoped it would just magically disappear."

Jackson laughed. "I almost believed you."

Walker gave his brother an indulgent look. "No joke."

"Well, I'll be damned." He made an obvious frown in Josie's direction. "You must not have settled that score yet. I see she is still sitting pretty."

"No, not yet. Now how should we go about this? There must be a connection somewhere. We just have to find it before something else happens."

The group decided Josie could work for as long as she wanted during the day if she didn't get a headache or was uncomfortable, but she couldn't walk the ranch alone nor leave alone. None of the women or children could. When she tried to explain why it would be easier for everyone if she left, both the younger Knight brothers and their wives gave Walker an expectant look, and he turned to give her a stern one.

"No one is going anywhere. We have not had that little follow-up conversation yet, but we will later tonight." Walker said in a matter-of-fact tone.

Jackson, the more demanding brother, said, "Well, make sure you do. She's a Knight for all intents and purposes, and Knights don't leave."

Josie scrunched up her face and then said, "Wait, didn't Piper and Camille leave for some years?"

"And they came back with consequences. We've learned from our mistakes. Besides, you were here several years ago and left, so you've had your time away. You're going nowhere, missy," said Walker.

"That's for damn sure," said Sawyer.

"Daddy said a bad word, mommy, he said..."

"Lily, we heard him. It isn't polite to point out the errors of grownups at the table."

Sawyer grinned. "Sorry, Piccadilly, now eat your dinner."

"Supper, daddy. Dinner is lunch. It's hard to remember, but you can do it."

The room roared with laughter at Lily's comment, breaking the tension.

Camille spoke up. "Now who's ready for dessert while we try to think why Josie being here is significant to someone when it wasn't the last time she was here."

A knock on the door gave Camille a chance to grab the pies and coffee while Piper put the older two in the playroom to eat their dessert in front of a favorite movie. Sawyer answered the door to the sheriff who'd stopped by to share what he had learned so far, which was a big, fat nothing.

"Can you all tell me again what happened with Corey. He isn't saying a thing."

"What about Renfro?" asked Jackson.

"Interesting thing, that. He said it's all Walker's fault, and right after he said it, he seemed to decide that was too much information and hasn't spoken a word on the subject since."

"He doesn't have any family nearby, so I don't imagine he's had any visitors," said Walker.

The sheriff took a sip of his coffee. "And there, you'd be wrong. A cute little thing, younger than Renfro, has come to visit him nearly every day since he took up residence in my jail. She offered to pay his bail, but it was more than she had collateral or cash for, so she has shown up every morning at ten, like clockwork. Name's Sherry Collins. Heard of her before?"

"Sherry Collins?" repeated Piper as she looked at Walker.

"Yes," said Walker. "She interviewed for the position that Josie has."

Randy sat up straighter, "Did she now?"

"So, he's friends with an applicant. While definitely interesting, it's not reason enough to initiate his actions," Sawyer said.

"Yeah, I'd agree, but they looked like more than just friends. I'd lay money on the fact that she is Renfro's girl," said Randy.

"And she doesn't live around here. She was several hours away, too much to drive every day and keep a job or anything," said Piper.

"And yet she is at the jail every day. Sorry, by the way, that they sent him back here. Something about overcrowding in the pre-adjudicated cases."

The room sat in silence as the inhabitants absorbed the information.

"So, you think Renfro was exacting revenge because his girl didn't get the job," said Jackson.

"I'd say so." The sheriff took another sip.

Josie sat up taller. "It makes a crazy kind of sense now that I think about it. Renfro said I shouldn't have gotten the job because I didn't know about the ranch or administrating one. He thought I hadn't worked on a ranch before. Now I see he was upset his girlfriend didn't get the job. But what about Corey?"

The sheriff stood to go. "Now, on that bit, I have no idea. I better be getting home, but I'll let you know if I hear anything, and you do the same." The men walked him out the door, and the women did what they needed to do to go to bed for the night.

The spanking that Walker initiated after Jackson took his family home and Sawyer took his own upstairs, was significant. Walker lectured, as typical, but he concentrated on the actual spanking, taking particular attention to covering each spot multiple times and leaving an indelible reminder of what her words meant. Josie was certain he had never been more serious about a lesson as he was now. It was a fact that he had never made his point more sharply than today, or maybe it was that she accepted it and didn't fight it because she wanted his words to be true to her.

"I. Love. You." Every word was punctuated by a stinging swat on a wiggling bottom. "Did you hear what I said? I love you. I am in love with you. That means you are precious to me. I've told you and tried to show you in as many ways as I could think of, but obviously, you need more because you haven't let it sink in, so we are covering that ground again. You belong to me as much as I belong to you."

He started on another round the world tour over her naked backside. The sharp sound of an enormous paw landing solidly on soft, buoyant flesh that rebounded after every smack, seemed to echo throughout the room. On and on, Walker lectured and reassured and on and on his hand landed on her upturned bottom.

The tears started, not because her rear end hurt, it did some, but Walker never put any of his strength into the swats, but it was the pain in her heart that nearly crushed her chest that had her weeping. Even though she was positive she'd cried out all her tears earlier in the day, a fresh round appeared fast on the heels of his demand that she be truthful to him and honest with herself. The rest would work itself out. Josie had her doubts, but she didn't dare voice them.

Walker had made sure she was supported on the bed and that the only part of her anatomy that was in danger of feeling any pain was her ass and that woeful region vibrated with heat when he was done. He bent down and kissed her salty lips and then the top of her head. The cozy feeling that came from that made her snuggle down in her bedding.

"That feeling you get that makes you want to burrow down in the warmth of that contentment, says you're surrounded in love and protection. It's the feeling of being part of a larger whole. A piece that fits perfectly in the puzzle and completes the picture. Only you can do that for me. I'm the only one who can do it for you. Now you need to let this all sink into your bones, into your very soul and take hold. I have some things I need to do, and then I'll come back, and we can make you feel better. Don't make me sorry I took compassion on you and gave you the benefit of the doubt."

"I won't, and Walker," he turned in her direction, "I'm in love with you, too."

"That's my girl. I'll be back soon."

And think she did. She lay on her tummy, finishing the last of her sniffles after Walker made no bones about what he thought of her decision to leave and her withholding her feelings from him and then lying about them. He left her to settle her aching bottom and do some thinking about being part of a family that held each person accountable in different, but significant ways. Could she do that? Learn to be part of this family? She hoped so.

Later, when Walker returned, he asked what she believed about the two of them. Josie said, "I believe we love each other, and that we can fix what we face as long as we do it together. I don't have to do everything alone, but I still want to sometimes. If a problem is too much, I can share the load and not be thought of as needy or incompetent. I'll be seen as part of a family unit that leans on each other."

"That all sounds nice and neat and tied up with a big bow, but how much do you really believe?"

"I believe all of it, but it's hard to change my habits of a lifetime, and it's even harder not to try to handle things alone because of those old insecurities that say I'll be less than respectable, less than worthy if I ask for help. I'll be a user. And unfortunately, I still believe it."

"That's okay, while you work on changing your thinking, it's my job to help you remember. Your job is to do your best to act on it as though you believe it all the time." His fingers slid through her tangled tresses and massaged her head. Josie loved that and thankfully, the tenderness was not as pronounced. "Now, about this needy girl I have right here..."

He drew her into him, his hands fisted in her silky strands and kissed her softly, gently tasting and inhaling her essence. Soon the need to go deeper took over his responses. His tongue traced her lips, which opened to his entreaty. Warm, wet, tasting of sweet minty chocolate, Walker mentally smiled. His girl was in the peppermint chocolates again. She loved those sweets. He was going to make her love this more.

She drew a deep breath and he plunged his tongue inside, twisting in a dueling fashion with hers, jabbing and sucking, tasting, melding, transforming. Josie pulled back and took another cleansing breath. He followed suit, pulling her shirt up as he exhaled.

"Raise your arms baby, it's time to get you naked."

Walker's warm fingers unhooked her bra as she threw off the top, tossing the lingerie in the same general direction. Searching hands reached for the snap and zipper of her jeans, his head dropped to her swollen breasts topped with taunting, jutting nipples just calling for his devouring.

Josie's whimpering increased as he drew in the first tightly ruched nipple into his mouth, sucking energetically, hungrily. Hands that appeared in his hair were drawn down through his short length and settled on his neck, then holding tightly to his corded muscles at the shoulders.

Josie was fully naked now. Walker raised his head from suckling her breasts and rasped, "This is my party, baby. You need to follow instructions this time. We are building your trust."

She immediately complied, her answer a whispered sigh made against his ear that sent a shiver of desire through him. He ravaged her lips a moment longer before standing and gathering items he might need.

"Lay back. Arms above your head and fingers clasped," he directed as his clothes came flying off.

He handled his erection, massaging it and cupping his own balls in gentle seduction. Pre-cum was perched precariously on the purple tip, and Josie whined.

"You want some of this, baby? Yeah, I want to share, but right now, you are sharing your body with me. Don't move your arms, this first part is mine. Spread yourself wide, sweetheart. Move your creamy thighs further apart. Yes, that will do."

A work-roughened finger slid through her wet valley, tracing the path from her hot sheath to her erect clit. Like his cock, it jumped when touched, reaching out for more contact, more friction. He circled her nerve button but didn't satisfy the need her clit begged for. Time enough for that. He drew his finger down through her wetness and further to her back hole, the forbidden doorway. Josie loved this playground, and he would be back for that bit of entertainment, but first, to start at the top.

His lips fell to her neck, licking, sucking, and kissing her soft, fragrant skin. Moving further south, he molded her breasts, bigger than his hands, into his grasp. Kneading one as he sucked the other, Josie began to writhe, bringing her legs up to encircle his waist so she could undulate her pelvis against his.

It was hot as hell and caused him to lose his concentration for a few seconds. He reached back and slapped her ass. Her cry of wanton need only heralded more frantic jostling of her sexy bits against his.

"Again." Josie was gasping as her breath quickened. Time for her first orgasm of the evening. His girl had many in her, so he didn't fear it would be premature to spill one now.

"Want more, baby? Look at me and don't look away. I want to see you ride this first wave.

Latching onto the other nipple, he sucked hard, drawing an angsty cry from Josie. "Yes, a little pain always helps you fly, baby. Need more?"

His hand rubbed her clit, giving only indirect pressure, then as she became frenzied, he slapped her butt once, twice. He allowed her nip to fall from his mouth as he leaned back to slap her ass and aim a full attack on her begging clit. One, two, three fast and furious swipes was all it took. Josie cried out her released ecstasy. On and on she flew as she continued to stare at him, her beauty bared for him to fall into.

As the first sparks of her flight faded, he brought her legs down from his waist and plunged into her pussy, forceful, violent as he felt her spasming muscles grip his cock, drawing it into her wet, vibrating sheath. Jabbing in and out, touching her womb, then he shifted again, changing his angle to hit her bumpy sensitive spot inside her pulsing sheath. She screamed as she shot off again, ricocheting from sizzle to sizzle as her ass clenched and her pussy grabbed at his staff. Pulling and arching, she brought her hands down to grab his ass and jerk him into movement.

Exiting her entrance enough to allow movement, Walker flipped her over, pulling her up to her knees. As soon as she comprehended what he needed, she helped position herself. His throbbing staff re-engaged, pumping quivering tissue where liquid arousal pooled. Taking some of her honey, he drew it up to her dark entrance. Her tight, dark backdoor contracted, hard.

Tapping his finger on her hole, he chastised, "Oh no, my dear, you will relax and let me in without forcing you. I want in, and you are going to welcome me."

Josie whimpered, but it was all an act. Walker learned early on that Josie was into ass play. She loved it. That's why spanking got her juices flowing and he intended that the next time she came, it would be with him. He wanted her hot and bothered; he'd be satisfied with nothing less than a scream. He tapped her brown entrance firmly with his finger.

She sighed a distressed but satisfied whine, allowing her to protest and release at the same time. His girl liked to protest what she actually wanted before giving in. But she would accept the inevitable and enjoy it. He added more of her hot, slippery, natural lubricant and slid his finger in as she moaned and softened.

Gaining a rhythm, he pumped his cock in her grabbing pussy, then plunged his finger, soon two fingers in her backdoor, and then scissoring them as he pulled them out only to delve in again. His cock was throbbing, painful, tight, and he felt the beginning of the burn. The hot rush of cum working its way to his cock and down the staff to engage his balls, tightening painfully.

The sizzle was moving down, down, through his pelvis, and he had to work fast. He stilled his movements and spread her lower lips wide, fully exposing her clit that stiffened at the sudden feeling of cooler air on its wet, hot surface. Finally, he began to fiddle with her nubbin, slamming into her pussy, doing his best to claim her hard while ramming his fingers into her ass, begging for her release.

Every part of him that could be, was engaged. He concentrated on her wild movements and activating all areas of ecstasy that he could while holding off his own nirvana for as long as he was able. It wouldn't be for much longer now, however. The pressure was building to volcanic proportions; pump, ram, tease, repeat. A fine sheen of sweat covered his body, his mind was numb with the pleasure that was at a peak level, and just when he didn't think he could hold out any longer, he pulled from her sheath.

Her cry of dismay and irritation that demanded she be refilled was met with silence as he squirted lubricant on his hot, pulsing cock. With a quick distribution and a directed squirt, he arranged his weapon of pleasure and pushed the enlarged, throbbing purple head with determined pressure. Through her sphincter muscle, he pressed his penis and continued with directed movements, his goal to bottom out. He did. She screamed and froze.

He picked up the dildo from beside him and shoved the almost too large toy partially into her pussy far enough to land on her spot that made her frantic with fear of peeing and the excitement of coming. Josie became frenzied. His effort to gain his own explosion took over, urging him to play with her hungry pussy with the toy up to the long, fat hilt and her anal entrance with his thrusting cock. Her devouring ass squeezed his cock hard, quivering with aftershocks of paradise won. Her clit was as erect as his cock, its sheath retracted, leaving its tender core exposed for more sweet torment.

Josie met as many movements as he would let her and her peak went on and on, her cries of delight and agony continued as he left her clit and released her filled pussy to take her hips and pound out his body's claiming of her.

His rush of relief shot hotly in her grasping core. A whole-body tremor signaled his final completion. Josie's chest was heaving, her breaths ragged as she tried to recover from her earth-shattering flight. Walker, too winded to do more than lean over his sweet girl and kiss her perspiring body under him.

"I love you." He said.

"I love you too. More than I ever thought possible."

After a few more minutes to get his feet under him, he said, "That was fun. Ready to go again?"

Josie laughed. "After I get a snack break."

"Naked?" he asked.

"Why not?" she said. Josie hoped she didn't regret it.

Chapter 15

Martin Acres was a 550-acre ranch that was largely un-used and had been since old man Martin had a heart at-tack five years ago but refused to leave the land he had farmed for most of his life. His son, Branch, tried to help but it was too much for a man who hadn't run the place since he left home at nineteen, nearly a decade ago. Branch Martin had grown up with Piper and the two older Knights. Camille and Sawyer were younger but remembered him. Josie was enamored with the quaint farm set up, and Walker was impressed with the amount of land and all that had been kept going even after Martin passed away six months ago.

"Branch, you've done an admirable job with the home-stead."

"Thanks, Walker, but I'm a real estate broker, not a rancher or farmer. This was too much for me to run, and the man I was going to hire seems to have gotten himself into a little trouble down your way."

"Renfro?"

"That's the one. He had his eye on the place, like you, and honestly, if Renfro had taken over the running of it and made a good go of it, I would have sold it to him for a percentage of the profits until he had paid the selling price off with interest. But I don't want to do business with a man who would attack without provocation. If you can't trust a man, then his word is no good."

"It shocked us as well. Have you met my Josie?"

"No, I haven't." Branch tipped his hat, "Pleasure, ma'am."

Josie laughed. "Josie, please."

"Josie, then. How'd you hook up with this guy, and how did I miss you?" Branch nudged Walker's shoulder only to get a nudge back.

"Hey there, that's dangerously close to hitting on my girl," said Walker, good-naturedly.

"I think you were in civilization when I was last here on Piper's ranch," answered Josie.

"Yeah, that sounds about right. This guy treating you well?"

She looked over at Walker contemplatively. "He is."

"Well, if that should change, let me know. I'll damn sure treat you right."

Josie laughed. Walker cleared his throat. "That's enough of that now. Branch, did Renfro know you were going to make him that deal?"

"No, he had asked if I'd hold on to the place for a while so he could come up with the down payment, and that's when I thought, if he could do the job, you know, I could make the deal, but we never discussed it."

"Did you tell him you'd wait?"

"No. What I did say was I had another offer on the table and needed to consider it as well."

"Did you tell him I was the other offer?"

"Didn't have to. Seems he already knew about your offer. Him and his girl wanted it. Seems like he thought she was going to work for you, but something fell through, I guess."

"I had interviewed her but didn't know she was Renfro's girlfriend. I wanted Josie for the job because we were together, but Josie had another job until right about then. I had already decided not to hire Sherry Collins."

"I thought her name was Colleen Shores?" said Branch.

"Oh. Could we be talking about different people?" asked Walker.

"I don't know, about five-seven, dark brown eyes, dark auburn hair, dresses nice like she'd never been on a ranch to work before?"

"Yep, that and a few other things were why I didn't consider her. Heels on boots for fashion on a working ranch is inexperience asking for trouble." Walker shook his head.

Josie looked down to peruse her attire. "Guess you're happy with the tired and worn fashion statement."

"Nah, I'm happy with the 'eyes for only me' look."

"Oh, well, then I think I have the competition beat."

"That you do, darlin'." Walker dropped a playful kiss on her lips before speaking to Branch. "I'm calling the sheriff's office when we're done here to let him know she has another name, and maybe that will tell us more about her. Now, I've got the cash for half and a guarantee for the other half, but we need to see the overall setup as the inspector, who just pulled up, looks over the house. Let's greet the man and then go check out what you have."

Five hours later, Walker and Branch shook hands. Branch settled the paperwork question. "I'll get the paperwork over to you accepting your offer this afternoon. Sometime tomorrow, I'll send over the contract. Thanks for working with me and not being one of those hard-nosed ranchers I normally work with on other's behalf. It seems that they know they wield power over those with less and push as hard as they can to get the most for the least. I always liked how you Knights were fair."

Late that afternoon, the offer and acceptance came through. The Knight men and Piper signed. Piper and Walker could cover a third of the investment, should the land not pay its own way in the next year. The next morning the contract was delivered, and as Walker was reviewing the 1.4-million-dollar agreement, the sheriff and his replacement knocked on the door.

"Hey, Sheriff, Randy, I didn't mean for you to come out here, or both of you. I'm honored. I would have talked on the phone."

"Yeah, I needed to stretch my legs and get out of the office for a bit," said the older man. "It was a good excuse."

"And I wasn't about to be left out of the loop on this one. It has me baffled," said Randy.

"Alright, then. Coffee?"

"Nah," said Randy, "I've had my fill for the morning."

The out-going sheriff shook his head. "No coffee, but you got any of Belinda's fresh orange juice?"

Walker laughed. "You bet. Randy?"

"No thank you. I'm all good."

"+I'll grab it. Just make yourselves at home."

Returning with a coffee refill for himself and juice for the sheriff, he sat down and asked his question to get a reaction from the men in front of him.

"Heard of a lady named Colleen Shores?"

The sheriff looked at Randy and then at Walker. "As a matter of fact, I have. What do you know, Walker?"

"Not sure, really. I got some interesting information yesterday. See, I was over at the Martin place finalizing the deal, and Branch and I got to talking about the place and..." Walker explained what he'd learned.

"Huh. I'll have to check this out, but if Colleen Shores and Sherry Collins are one and the same, it could explain a lot. A lot." The sheriff stood and polished off the juice. "Best juice in the state."

"I'll tell Belinda when she gets back from town. It'll make her day."

"Walker, keep this under your hat."

"I already spoke to my family, but they knew I was coming to you with the information."

"Well, if this is what I think it is, you dodged a bullet by not hiring Renfro's girlfriend, Sherry Collins or Colleen Shore or whoever she is. And Renfro might have dodged one by being in my jail right now. I'll get back with you soon."

The two men talked as they stood on the porch. "Oh, and Walker, keep your women and children in sight until I get back with you, if possible."

"It's possible," said Walker, giving Josie a stern look.

"And glad to see you doing better, Miss Josie."

"I think we are all healing up but I hope we can settle this whole business and get on with living soon."

"Yes, ma'am. We'll do what we can to make that happen."

The men shook hands, and the incoming and outgoing sheriff climbed into the truck and drove off.

"That the sheriff or a deputy driving off?" asked Sawyer.

"Sheriff, both of them. Come on into the office. I have to get Jackson on the line. There's something brewing."

"THAT IS RIDICULOUS. If he can't tell us why we need to be extra careful, I have things that I can't put off," complained Josie as she stood with her hand resting on Walker's forearm in the family room. Walker did not seem impressed.

"Nevertheless, you will put them off or wait until one of us can go with you. Josephine Rodriguez, until we get more information and you get the okay from me, you do not go anywhere without one of the guys or me. Not on or off the ranch. I do mean anywhere."

She dropped her hand, a look of distaste on her face. "I hate that name, and I hate not being free to do what I want to do, what I need to do."

Walker leaned down and kissed Josie on the lips before landing a warning swat to her butt. He pulled her close and laid his cheek on top of her head.

"And I hate that you might not be safe at home, but you'll hate it more if you don't do as I say. That saucy little ass will be fire engine red and carry a burn that no amount of ice will cool." He lifted his head and leaned her back from his embrace to make eye contact. "I mean business here, woman. I love you. That makes me a force to be reckoned with, and never doubt I will do all I can to keep you and the others safe."

Josie stepped back to look fully into his eyes. "I know." Her hand slid down his cheek. "But I can handle taking care of myself. I've done it my whole life." Josie warmed to her subject, her words gaining in volume, the bite returning to her words. "What am I supposed to do while I wait for someone to follow me around? It is ludicrous. I won't do anything that would endanger myself, knowingly. You know that."

Walker frowned again and turned her around to lead her outside and back toward the office. His hold was firm and somehow reassuring. Her irritation was not waning, however, and Josie stomped up the stairs to the room above the supply barn, complaining at every step. She repeated her last argument as they neared the top of the stairs.

"Do I know that you will do what is necessary to stay safe? I hope so, but there is no way in hell that I or the others will risk their family on the illusion that we are as safe as we were before this mess. Go back over the contract for the numbers and do some projections on the profitability of this buy. Do separate ones on the livestock and the farm stock. Then, go over my numbers and see if I missed anything on the first two years operational costs and profits. If you get really bored, go over the house inspector's recommendations for repairs and make a list of what you want for your new home."

Josie sat hard in her desk chair in the ranch office, moving things around on the desk while grumbling. "I don't see what the big deal is. Even if this Sherry and Colleen are the same people, who cares?"

"The sheriff, and since he's the one who asked that you women not go anywhere alone, it isn't just me being overprotective. It applies to all females and children, so stop acting like you are being targeted for unfair treatment. I expected better from you."

Josie's shoulders slumped. "I know. I just had my whole week planned out now that I'm back to normal." She smiled wryly. "After I was convinced to stay, that is, and it feels like the universe is against me by stopping me from doing just that."

"I don't know about the universe, but I'm putting a halt to it right now. Remember, salsa."

Josie laughed. "Lemonade, silly."

"Texas, remember?"

"Whatever." She laughed and rolled her eyes. "Go on and get back to whatever you're doing today, and I'll get you some projections. Then I'll get going on a list of how you can spend some of your money on what I want in the house, starting with the repairs."

The relief showed clearly on Walker's face. He dropped a long, slow kiss on her mouth, savoring the touch. Pulling back, he spoke with their lips millimeters apart. "Thanks, honey. I promise we'll get to the bottom of this soon."

She stole a kiss. "You'd better. Now shoo so that I can spend your money, at least on paper."

Walker laughed as he stepped back. "Maybe I need to put a limit..."

"That ship has sailed, cowboy. I know what your balance sheet says." He laughed with her.

Josie was as good as her word and tackled the projections, finding she was surprised at the outcomes. That piece of land was a good buy with two ponds fed underground by the Clearwater River that also fed the Clearwater Gentry Ranch and the Clear Knight ranch. There appeared to be plenty of grazing land, but the existing cattle were about average. Jackson would need to add an influx of superior bull stock so that they could increase the salability of the beef. It might take a few years to see any profitable return, but in the meantime, it could sustain itself. That was enough.

Dinner that night was centered around the ranches. Jackson and Piper decided to have a night in, so the conversation was less lively without those two.

Camille asked, "Any news from the sheriff?"

"No news," answered Walker. "I imagine he is checking his facts before calling us back. I'll give him a ring in the morning to find out. So, what did you do today, Camille?"

"Not nearly what I had intended."

"Cami," was all the warning Sawyer uttered.

"Well, it's so frustrating. Just give me a handgun and let me do what I need to do. You know I can shoot."

"You're trained, not tried," mumble Sawyer.

"Hey," said Josie, perking up at the idea, "That would be a great solution. After dinner, we can get them and test them out in the field. I have a couple of small caliber ones that are just perfect for..."

"No," said Sawyer.

"They are my guns, Sawyer," said Josie.

"No, you aren't bringing them out for protection," said Walker.

"Why?" asked Camille. She gave a hard look at her husband. "And not because you said so. A real reason."

Sawyer answered, "Because you haven't had enough chance to get used to them and because every hand on this ranch has a firearm right now. You don't need one."

"And," said Walker with a grin, "Because I said so." Josie opened her mouth, "Don't even try it, young lady. That offer this morning is still valid. Besides, I hid the ammo."

"You what?" Josie sat back, clearly preparing for battle when she looked around the room and her shoulders suddenly slumped. "Then you had better figure this out fast, mister, because I have a finite amount of patience."

Walker sighed. "I know, baby. Thank you for hanging in there. Both of you." His look encompassed Camille as well. "I'll do what I can tomorrow." The weight of the situation on Walker was evident.

Josie didn't want to add to his weight. She knew she had gold in her hand and wouldn't trade it for any amount of freedom. "Good. We trust that you are all doing what you can. Now let me tell you what I think about the projections you wanted."

After they discussed the house, the land, the ideas, sent the kids on their way to play and put the baby down, they continued to plan. By the time they had exhausted the subject, Sawyer and his gang went upstairs, and Walker and Josie headed for the cottage. They missed being able to raise the roof when they made love. Josie knew that Walker needed to show her a good time tonight as a reward. She encouraged it. She wanted a good time. She imagined Sawyer felt the same with Camille.

The light had gone, and Josie was fresh from her shower, relaxed and warm. The days were warm enough, but the nights had retained a distinct briskness. She loved this weather. And she loved being in love. It made even the situation they were facing bearable. She laid on the bed, towel still wrapped around herself, and picked up her tablet. She enjoyed reading but had very little time to do more than read the stock reports, projection sheets, and almanac these days.

Soon she was fully engrossed in her novel when there was a tickle at her toes. She wiggled them and encountered only air, so she returned to her book. Next, she felt a tickle up her leg, light, barely there, suggesting visions of a scorpion or another creepy-crawly as she jumped from the bed swatting at whatever it was. The bug was huge. It was brown with bulging muscles and stood six foot two with laughing eyes.

"What the hell," Josie asked, but she couldn't help but laugh. He was holding a feather and wiggled it in the air.

"I heard women liked a little teasing touch. I thought a feather would be light enough."

She laughed. "Walker, they mean in sex, not in ambush."

"I could do a sexy ambush."

"Well, this wasn't it, babe."

"No? Well, let me try again."

Walker pinned her to the wall, causing her womb to clamp down hard on itself, empty and lacking companionship. She didn't want sweet and easy, she wanted hot and hard. As his lips descended on hers, Josie took control and bit his lip, running her tongue over it to soothe the pinch, but it was enough to tell him this one would be fast and furious.

"I gotcha sweetheart. Hold on."

His mouth crashed onto hers, bruising and seeking gratification. Tongues tangled, and a reenactment of the mating dance was initiated in her mouth. He was inside her: jabbing, sucking, rubbing, taking, giving, energizing, exhausting. His lips then moved to her neck and shoulder, nipping, licking, tickling, biting, as he squeezed her plump breasts, pinched her nips and tugged on them just to the point of pain. He rolled the tips between his thumb and forefinger, both globes simultaneously, before latching onto one quickly before moving to the next with his hot wet mouth.

"Climb me." She did.

Lifting her thighs, she wrapped herself around his waist and pulled him closer. Their breath mingled; their perspiration shared. His cock was diamond hard as she reached to hold his sac gently and firmly squeezed. His anguished cry made her gush with liquid need. Her ears were full of the whoosh of blood pumping through her veins.

"Mount me."

She positioned her wet opening in front of his throbbing cock, then she impaled herself with the cock-sword. She was so wet he nearly slid back out, but she rearranged herself and slammed down as he jabbed up. When the connection hit her womb, she felt her inner walls clamp down on him as he drove in and out while holding her in place against the wall. Hard, fast, furious, and so damn hot, the pleasure was mind-numbing.

"Let go. Come, baby."

He leaned down to nibble her tit and then claimed her mouth with his, tongues doing battle as he continued to claim her. Suddenly, the moment was upon her. The rush of sensation overpowered her, forcing Josie to release a scream, holding on for fear of falling into the abyss of pleasure forever and somehow knowing one wouldn't survive so much intensity. He bit her shoulder, and his sword quivered, fattened, and then exploded, his sizzling essence coating her insides and rolling hot and steamy down her thighs.

Josie was in bed when she came down from that incredible flight. Walker was lying half on her and said, "We didn't use anything."

"Do you care?" Her question was only partially thought out.

"Hell no, but we haven't talked about it."

"Later." Rolling over to kiss his fine lips, she could tell she would be bruised. His hands supported her, gripping hard at her waist and hips. She loved it.

"Hurting?"

"I will be."

"Here, I'll kiss and make it better."

Chapter 16

Sitting in her office chair the next morning, Josie was still feeling as though she was skating on the sexy high Walker gave her last night. After the third time, she was too exhausted to do more than close her eyes and sleep. She was still delightfully tingly, but not stinging like when he was making an ass statement. It was a warm sparkle that he'd reignited as Walker slowly brought her off before getting in the shower this morning. Josie loved this man more than she had ever thought possible, and not just because he was good in bed, although that was nothing to shake a stick at. Josie loved all aspects of him, well, except when he was super bossy like now. She smiled to herself; he was teachable, though.

"I need to sit down with Piper today and go over some numbers with her. I'm taking the new ranch projections with me to help us figure out the next move. She's swamped, so I'm going to her. Will you be okay here? I don't want you to go anywhere except this office and the main house. Got it? No exceptions."

"I won't go anywhere alone, I promise. Have you gotten in touch with the sheriff's office?"

"He was out of the office but will call me when he gets back."

"Okay, fine." She closed the filing cabinet a little harder than she had intended, but Walker didn't seem to notice. "But as soon as the buddy system is over, you'll let me know, right? As soon as."

Walker laughed. "Yes, ma'am." He dropped a panty-melting kiss as he massaged and squeezed her bottom. "Mmm. I'll be back for more of this." One more quick kiss before he strode out of the office as though he owned the world. He did. His corner of it, anyway.

Josie was just finishing her comparison shopping for the front door to their new home when the phone rang. The only time anyone called the ranch was for business. Anyone wanting something else knew the family well enough to call their cell phones or the house phone. She put on her professional voice and answered.

"Good morning, Clear Knight Ranch."

"Hey, it's Branch, Branch Martin. Can I speak with Walker, please?"

"Hi, this is Josie. Sorry, Walker is out for a while. Is there anything I can do, or can I take a message?"

"Well, I promised him the appraisal results, and they just came in. I'd email them, but I have a paper version that I printed off for him. I thought I'd be able to drop it off, but I'm not going to have the time. I know he wants it as soon as he can get it.."

"I have a copy of the appraisal right here."

"That was the preliminary before Walker asked for some additional bits in it. This is the final version."

"Can you just email it?"

"I don't have access to the file right now on email. I don't have my computer. I'm out here at the place, working on the personal inventory removal. I can hang out here for a little while if you want to come and get it."

"Um, I'm not sure I can." Couldn't he email it or snap a photo of it? Was his cell phone ancient, and did his real estate office not have a computer? There was an unease about this whole thing. "We can wait until you get back to your office later."

"It will be tomorrow. I'm not going in today. Well, don't worry. I'm sure I can get him a copy in a day or two. It's just that I know he needs it to finish his closing paperwork."

"Okay, well, I'll get there soon." She bulldozed past the inner voice and committed.

"That sounds great. I'll wait." But wasn't he busy?

"I can be there in about twenty minutes."

"Oh, I'm at the ranch house."

"Okay, that's closer. Give me about fifteen."

Josie headed out the door after grabbing a ranch hand to go with her. Running inside to let Camille know where she was going and with a hand. Josie stopped to write a quick note for Walker. She didn't allow the feeling of foreboding to interfere with getting the information for closing. She thought he had already closed, but she didn't really know much about these things. So, if he needed it, he needed it. She was glad for the opportunity to feel productive again. She decided to give Walker a quick call, frowning when it went to voicemail. She said she wasn't alone and to call her or Camille for details.

"How long have you worked for the ranch?" she asked conversationally as they were driving away from the property.

"Me? I don't work for the ranch. Branch just asked me to hang around and offer a ride to someone that matched your description."

"But we're in one of the Clear Knight trucks. How'd you get it?"

"You handed me the keys. And I was dropped off." That voice. It sounded so familiar.

She felt the panic rise. "How were you supposed to offer me a ride if you didn't have a vehicle?"

"Well, you made that easy, didn't you?" The man was rough around the edges, but Josie couldn't decide if he was intelligent and keeping his cool or stupid and didn't see it was a situation that would soon cause him a great deal of trouble.

"Where are you taking me?" she swallowed hard to keep the bile down.

"To Branch's place, like you asked me to."

"You mean as Branch asked you to."

The man nodded his response but didn't offer his name, nor did he do any more talking, just pulled up in front of Branch Martin's farm. He parked, hopped out, and left the keys in the truck as he meandered away without another word. What the... No, something was very wrong. Josie decided to slide over and drive back home. She tried to call Walker as she attempted to move over to the driver's side.

"Walker, when you get this, I need help. I..."

A female voice behind her spoke. "Hang up, Miss Rodriguez." Josie froze. "Now!" the woman yelled.

Thinking quickly and speaking even faster, Josie said, "Martin. Help. Hurry." Instead of hanging up completely, she quickly tapped on the record app as she hung up from Walker's voicemail. Josie was proud of her ability to know her phone and apps so well, she knew where to go for important things without looking. As in this case, when she used her phone to record things that she would need to recall later.

She brought the phone down and asked. "Who are you?"

"I wanted to formally meet you before, well... I'm Colleen Shores; you might know me as Sherry Collins. And you are the infamous Josie. The woman who has destroyed so much because she refused to be run off her boyfriend's ranch. I have to say I admire your tenacity, sticking it out even after that last knock on the head."

"What do you mean? How do you know about that? Was it you?"

"Oh, yes, that was me. It was like trying to get into Fort Knox by then. Everyone had weapons and showing them as they carefully watched everything. Ranches are notorious for being easy to get in and out of, but not here. I'm sure it had to be a bit confusing with the puppy dog Corey in this mess with your boyfriend, and yet the only one they had to blame for the knot on your head. I wasn't sure you'd survive that, but you have an exceptionally hard head, Josie. Too bad it won't help you survive now. Bullets are notorious for being disrespectful of one's determination to survive." Colleen, aka Sherry's face, contorted. "Toss that phone. You won't need it on our adventures." Josie dropped it at her feet.

"So, what are you doing at Branch's place?"

"My ranch, you mean? Mr. Martin has been so good as to accept my offer."

"But Walker already bought it. The Clearwater Ranches own it now or close enough. You can't offer for it. The sale supposed to be signed several hours ago...completed this morning." She had no idea if that was true or not, but it sounded good and finished.

The fury that met Josie's statement froze her in fear. "He did! He had no choice, obviously, but he has accepted it!"

Josie went into survival mode. Don't incite. Keep your surroundings in your mind when searching for a way out. Don't be a hero. *No chance of that.*

"Is that a 9mm handgun? I hear it packs a punch."

It worked. Colleen shrugged almost nonchalantly. "I can handle it." Suddenly remembering what she was supposed to be doing, the manic woman stepped out of the doorway. "Now, get out of the truck." What did this Collins/Shores chick want with her?

"I think I should go home. Walker is expecting me."

"No, he isn't. He is in town with Piper Gentry. That bitch seems to own everything in and out of town. The Midas touch, I hear. It will come in handy."

"Why? Look, you can't hurt Piper. She has a child."

"That has no bearing on whether I can hurt Piper Gentry Knight, but I won't need to. I have you, and since Walker's woman is everything to him, he'll back out of this property right away to save your scrawny neck."

"You are going to use me to make Walker trade the property for me? But I don't understand. If it is already recorded, there has to be a new appraisal, a new inspection, everything. And the state doesn't allow the sale of property that is less than a price within a small range of the value. You need a closer, and they verify these things. It's even been renamed. Look, if you want a piece of property, there are plenty of places you could have. Why Martin Acres?"

"Ranch. It's a ranch."

"On the paperwork, it said, never mind. Why do you want the ranch?"

"Walker was going to buy it, and he didn't tell you the importance of it?"

"The land is great for grazing cattle and growing farm animals. We are going to live in the house if the report comes back that it's sound enough. The outbuildings are..."

"None of those things matter. You really are tiresome like Adam was. He preferred to be called Renfro, can you believe it? That's as boring as he is, as you are. He didn't seem to know what the significance of the property was at first, either. No, I want the treasure."

"Treasure? There's no treasure." It was obvious Josie thought Colleen had lost her mind, and that seemed to amuse the woman.

"You think I'm crazy, but I'm cleverer than the rest of you backroad dirt eaters. In the cave on the edge of the property, there's gold. I've seen it. I know of others who will swear to the precious metals and stones in there."

"Like whom?"

"My parents. That surprises you, doesn't it? My parents used to work on the ranch before I was born. When I was growing up, they would tell me the stories. There are Old West and Spanish relics that would be worth a pretty penny now. Things made of gold and silver in a small cave at the back corner of the ranch."

"You say you've seen it?"

Colleen's head nodded animatedly. "Oh, yes. Right in the wall, running in lines, veins, I think they call it. The place sparkles."

Josie's voice was gentle but unemotional. "Why do you think this place wasn't teeming with offers, then? Why didn't Branch just mine it himself or his dad?"

"Maybe they didn't know."

"Didn't know that for generations, they had precious stones and metals on their land, but others did? That doesn't sound right."

"Shut up!" Colleen was showing signs of doubt, which made her anger become more unpredictable.

Time to stop poking the bear. "Where is this treasure again?"

"The cave on the backend of the property, but don't get any ideas."

"I think I know where you're talking about. Walker said that every kid thought they had found gold, but it was just iron pyrite. Fool's gold. Don't ruin your life for fool's gold."

Colleen swung her gun around. "Shut up. You don't know what you're talking about. My parents wouldn't lie."

Josie looked confused, exaggerating the expression for Colleen's benefit. *Act ignorant.* "But this property didn't come with the mineral rights. The owner retained the rights. He deeded the water but not the mineral rights." The angry sounds that came from the woman were frightening, even to Josie, who thought it wouldn't take much to change the course of things. "Lots of people have their mineral rights deeded separately.

Colleen Shores picked up Josie's phone and glanced at it. "Listening in? Good. Walker Knight, I have your woman. Give me the deed, and I'll give you your woman. It's a fair trade."

"He won't get that. It's on a recording, but you have to send it to him before he can get it."

The woman showed her growing agitation and swung her gun in Josie's direction. "Send it, then toss the phone in the truck. We have someone waiting for us." Evidently, she was done with disclosures.

Branch, who was guarded by the man who had driven Josie here, met them in an outbuilding Walker planned to use for newborn animals as needed. "Branch, are you okay?"

"I'm so sorry, Josie, they made me. I didn't call for you, but when Walker wasn't there, and you offered, *she*," he raised his chin to indicate Colleen, "jumped at the chance to have you to hold over Walker."

"But how did you get here?"

Branch Martin shook his head in anger. "I was duped into coming to sign a paper that this woman said I had missed. It needed to be completed to finish the purchase. I thought she was a new person from the title company. What it actually turned out to be was to sign a transaction she had drawn up in her name, Colleen Shores."

Colleen took up the information. "Yes, and when he got here, I found out Walker Knight had slipped in front of me and stole this land." She ended the sentence in a foiled villain's voice from some superhero movie. The odd mania was alarming.

"But maybe I was wrong, and they haven't signed yet," said Josie.

Branch nodded his head. "Everyone did, so I recorded this morning."

"What? It's ours?" asked Josie. She changed her demeanor. "Oh, good. I thought they said they did, but I was busy last night with Walker, so I didn't pay attention to any business conversation." The implication was clear, and while it was unnecessary, it was an attempt to throw her off track.

"Guess you aren't in the loop as much as you think. Your boyfriend has already finished the sale." Colleen said in a jeering voice. "When I told Mr. Martin what he needed to do to end this whole thing, you know what he said?" Again, the tone was hateful and mocking. "He said, 'You know I recorded the deed this morning, right? I can't sell you what I don't own. I'm sorry, I can't help you.'"

Branch nodded grimly. "It's true. When I got the call, I worried that we had put the cart before the horse, so I had to deal with it immediately."

"But what about Renfro and Corey?" asked Josie. She needed to stall, but she also wanted the rest of the story.

"What about them?" The woman had no remorse.

"How are they part of this, and why?"

"Because they're stupid men, that's why. You are asking the dumbest... Oh, I get it. You are hoping lover boy makes it soon enough to save the day."

Colleen Shores raised her gun. Josie closed her eyes tight, remembering the pain that being knocked out had caused. Expecting to hear the crack of the gun over Branch's head, she waited, but instead, Colleen shot at him. Once she realized the active danger they were in, Josie was trying to locate Colleen because the woman wasn't afraid to shoot. The good thing was, the firearm did have a helluva kick, knocking Colleen off balance some. It was enough for Josie to bump the gun and misdirect any next shot, but the gun went off again as Josie's kidnapper hit the ground.

There was an immediate grunt just as Josie hit the ground on her knees hard. She had to get away from the barn, this crazy woman, the whole situation, and quickly, or she would be the next casualty. She prayed the grunt she heard wasn't from Branch Martin.

Josie needed to see if Colleen had hit anyone. Still on her knees, Josie tried to reorient, but before she could, there was answering gunfire followed by shouts of outrage and what sounded like a herd of stampeding wild horses. Josie opened her eyes to chaos. Strong arms wrapped around her, yanking her to her feet, and propelled her to the door at a speed that she had no time to do more than stay upright.

All she knew was to fight like hell if she was to get away alive. No matter what was happening, she had to survive, get to the truck, to Walker. Sweaty arms tightened around her waist; hot breath washed over her cheek.

"It's me, woman. Quit kicking and fighting me. Baby, it's me, Walker." A voice was breaking through her thoughts, familiar. "Dammit, never mind, just run. Hurry."

Chapter 17

Randy Cambridge, the newly installed sheriff, looked at the full living room at the Clear Knight. "Okay, you yahoos, I need to get some clarification. Joe said he tried to finish this out for you all and was sorry he wasn't here at the final unveiling to put the last bit of the puzzle together with you, but his plane for his daughter's place left today." Randy clapped his hands and then rubbed them together like he was about to settle into Thanksgiving Dinner. He grinned at the room. "So, you have me. You start, and I'll fill in what I know as it arises."

Walker looked at his family gathered around him and took a sip of his iced tea as his arm came out from around Josie's waist to settle in for his part of the information sharing.

"Okay, get your pen out because I'm going through this quickly. I've had enough rehashing of this mess to last me for a lifetime. There is a little backstory that I'll throw in first. Josie and I have been an item off and on for nearly three years now. I wanted her to take the assistant job, to work with me for almost a year, but it hasn't worked out for one reason or another until the beginning of last month."

"Walker, people don't need to rehash our private lives," Josie spoke quietly but firmly. She was learning from Walker that a quiet tone and calm manner worked best to get your point across.

He patted her knee. "That's all the background needed, baby. It helped to fill in the rest. Anyway, I've been looking for a ranch for some time to do the bulk of the administration from and possibly to settle down on my own spread. It would also give Josie a place of her own, and each of us would have a spread to work from, our main operation, you know? We work these two as divisions of the same ranch, and mine would be more of farming for the family's needs kind of set up, with some exotics and whatever else we thought might bring a profit."

"Okay, so then you made a deal with Branch," said Randy.

"Yes. After we held off a while, but then negotiated a tentative price. It would be finalized after we set up the inspection and appraisal and ran some numbers. As soon as Branch and I were ready to finalize the sale, we would. The paperwork was being drawn up but not dated. We were waiting for the appraisal and inspections to finish the numbers."

"Then why did Renfro think he was going to buy it?" Randy asked as he busily wrote notes.

"I imagine because it had been sitting for so long, the housing and some of the outbuildings would have to be redone. It would go for a cheaper price, and the for sale sign didn't say sold. Technically, it wasn't yet, but the agreement was in place. I guess you could say it was under contract but not until recently. And honestly," said Walker." I wouldn't have looked again so soon if Ms. Collins hadn't been so interested in that place during the interview. It had been priced too high for the fair market value when I checked some time before. Branch was feeling out the interest and saw it wasn't as favorable as he had hoped. Which is when we struck our tentative deal."

"And Renfro never asked?" The perplexed lawman asked.

"Randy, I'm honest when I tell you we don't know why. You would have thought he'd have stayed on top of it," said Jackson.

"All I know is he wanted to purchase that ranch for Colleen Shores, aka Sherry Collins, the woman who had applied for the assistant job with Walker for the ranches, but Walker didn't hire her," added Piper.

"Right," continued Walker. "Renfro wanted his woman to be hired so she could feed him the records and business information he needed to cripple the ranch enough to allow him to slip in and buy the Martin Place. He'd saved, but not enough for the down payment. If I were distracted, then it wouldn't be my priority."

Randy added more. "Corey explained to me that Renfro promised that he could learn to be the foreman if he did what Renfro needed. When Walker talked about moving on that property and started the purchase negotiations, the wait that Renfro was hoping on, was over. He needed to put Walker off focusing on the buy and onto other things, like his own sweetheart."

"Yes, when Walker didn't hire Renfro's girlfriend, he got greedy and worried, so he started all that mess here at the ranch," said Sawyer. "He had a deal of sorts with Branch to run the ranch, show a profit and that profit and work would go into paying off the property and Branch would have eventually sold to him."

"But then got himself in my jail," said Randy.

"Right, and that was when Renfro's sweetheart went solo," said Jackson. "And Branch decided it wasn't a deal that would happen."

"Yes," said Josie. "She thought there was a treasure in the cave on the property like her parents had entertained her with stories of, and she refused to believe that it wasn't true. Fool's gold convinced her the stories were true."

"Most likely. Anyway, I think that's it in a nutshell," said Walker.

"Yep," said Sawyer, "A real piece of work."

"Well, since I have arrested Ms. Shores, the men have opened up, all of them. What happened, according to Renfro, went something like this. She figured she'd get Renfro to purchase the property, then she would find the treasure and leave him with the mortgage, but then it was his idea for her to get a job at the ranch. That way, she would be close to him and the negotiations on the ranch. At first, it seemed like a good idea to find out what else was in the area that she could lay her hands on, but Walker didn't hire her."

"She didn't seem right for the job," said Walker.

"Thank goodness for your instincts," said Jackson.

Randy continued. "Well, then there had to be a change of plans when Josie showed up. They decided to work on getting rid of Josie and possibly reintroduce Sherry. Or at least draw his attention away so they could swoop in and buy it first. Then Renfro got arrested because the fool couldn't get past the fact that Walker didn't hire his girlfriend when he had it set up so well. He showed his hand too easily. Sherry decided it was time to ditch Renfro as soon as she could find out what he knew. Evidently, Renfro tried one last time to gain his girl's affections or whatever. He got the kid to do his dirty work. You know all that part."

Sawyer jumped in. "But when it was obvious everything was going south fast, why didn't they just stop?"

"Greed. When Corey was arrested, Ms. Shores wasn't willing to let go of the plan, so she decided just to steal and leave. You gotta feel a little sorry for Renfro. He really thought she was going to work the ranch with him. Corey was going to be the manager, and they would live happily ever after. But they hadn't factored in the background of Shores because they didn't know it. Didn't do any research."

Josie spoke quietly. "If you lie with crooks, you die with crooks. Not quite appropriate in this case, but Renfro sure is stuck doing some real time. Corey was a tool. And those two goons she had with her at the Martin place."

"And all for a legend that wasn't true," said Jackson.

"That about sums it up." Randy leaned back in his seat.

"No, who ran me off the road? Who was in the office and why?"

"Ah," said Randy, "that was another person she hired. He was a petty thief that she scrounged when Corey found himself in hot water with the law. He was to scare you off, and if it caused an accident that you didn't recover from, seeing you still had that arm injury, all the better. I imagine he was looking for anything that might be part of the sale. He showed up to get paid, and we nabbed him."

"So he wasn't the one who was waiting for me to go to the farm."

"Nope, just reminded you of him, I guess. Now, what about this new ranch? Branch was telling the truth. You have bought it, right?" Randy leaned back into the armchair.

"Yes. The Clearwater Gentry and Clear Knight ranches now have a third ranch," said Sawyer.

Randy asked. "So, what are you going to call it?"

"I've been thinking about that," said Walker. "We are in negotiations for some rescue animals, and who knows what we will end up doing besides what we have already started. Bison for Josie, mustangs for Sawyer, beef for Jackson, and farm animals for teaching the kids. But I bought it to give Josie a refuge. Someplace that is hers, where she can do whatever is feasible and know that she will be the one offering to help others instead of how it was during her childhood. We are going to ultimately have a small summer camp to help kids build their trust and self-esteem."

Piper spoke up. "Well, it has to have Clear in the name, as these two ranches do in honor of our river that runs through, providing our water."

Walker and Josie looked at each other and smiled. "So, how does the Clearwater Refuge sound?"

"Absolutely perfect," sighed Camille. No one disagreed.

"Okay, and one more announcement. Just to let you know, Josie and I will be getting married around Christmas." The room burst into joyous laughter and animated chatter.

Josie looked at the man she loved through the chaos and knew any disagreement with this part of his plan would not sit well with him. He was high-handed again, and she could feel her bottom twitch with the argument that it was too soon to contemplate marriage until she realized it didn't matter.

She wanted that with Walker. The children, the property, and the house with the white picket fence. And this time, she was going to make sure she was the one offering, not taking. It felt good to know she could pay back good people and erase all of those bad memories, making them good.

Yes, this time, Walker's high-handedness was all right with her.

EPILOGUE

One Year Later:

Josie, Camille and Piper sat next to the Clearwater Creek that ran through their properties, indulging in their monthly family picnic. This time, they were gathered on Walker and Josie's homestead. They had been working on the property for a year, and except to take a week to honeymoon in Alaska, they had been hard at it for twelve months. Today was the official end of all the projects.

The section of land surrounding the house was laid in lush St. Augustine grass enclosed in that white picket fence that Josie had balked at not much more than a year before. The walkway extended to the fence gate guarded by two Aussie pups. Walker had begun to put in some time training them to corral livestock and children as needed. The rest of the Refuge lay beyond that white gate, and that was where Walker and Josie split responsibilities.

Piper and Camille plied Josie with questions as the children played nearby, and the men tossed horseshoes with high stakes of chores and bragging rights.

Piper sat up excitedly. "Hey, I forgot to tell you that Jackson was asked to speak at a Cattleman's Conference at Texas A&M."

"What's he going to talk about?" asked Josie.

"His breeding schedule and method. He will be one of three speakers who have two hours each to talk about what they do. The conference is for two days. Jackson figures he will get some business out of it. The exposure will also give credence to his expertise in this area of cattle."

"What an honor. He's going to put Clearwater Ranch on the map," said Camille.

Piper looked over where the men were horsing around more than tossing horseshoes. "He is so excited."

"He should be." Josie turned to Camille. "Now, did I hear something from Walker about Sawyer being asked to help with a Mustang run?"

"Oh, right. He got a call from the land management people a few days ago. They asked him if he would mind helping them save some of a herd of wild mustangs that are in danger of being destroyed. He can take all he wants and can re-home them."

"Wow, how did they get his name?" asked Piper.

"I think Walker had something to do with it when he was asking the State about using Mustangs for the children to ride. He talked Sawyer's abilities up, and one thing led to another. It's something to be asked, and the profit at re-homing would be a huge boost." Camille looked for Sawyer along the river's edge before smiling. "Since we will have another mouth to feed in about seven months."

"What?"

"Congratulations."

The women spoke excitedly about the newest little Knight on his or her way. "We aren't telling the children yet, so don't spill the beans."

Josie raised her head and glanced at the men, watching them slapping Sawyer on the back. He took Camille's cue, obviously.

Piper turned to Josie. "Now, tell us about your news."

"Oh, well, we don't really have any yet. We don't know if we will get the license or not, but it looks like we will, and then the fun begins."

Camille tickled her toddler as he played on the blanket. "But don't you want a child of your own?"

"Who says we won't have one later, or we could adopt? But right now, bringing foster children to a place like this will be incredible. We want short-term ones at first, so we will do emergency placements to allow for a safe hiding place for those who need it. In a few years, when we are ready, we will do the camp. In the meantime, we have offered foster children an opportunity to come and pet the animals, learn about a farm and ride ponies. We will do it once a month, starting with a few hours later this afternoon."

Josie's eyes lit up when she spoke about becoming a foster parent and sharing the world with children who needed a glimpse of hope.

"I have to say that it was incredible to watch the guys pick out ponies for this afternoon," said Piper. "You know the horses all have different personalities, and they think differently."

"Well," clarified Camille, "except they all think like men." The women laughed.

Piper continued. "Yes, well, other than that shared flaw, Jackson was all about the sturdiness and breeding." She mimics her husband's deep voice. "'It has to be surefooted.' Sawyer was about the pony's gentleness, their amiability and patience." She changed her voice to a more instructional tone. "'He can't be a biter. That would ruin everything.' Now, Walker. He was the best of all. He said it had to pass the Josie Test."

Josie laughed. "What is the Josie Test?"

Piper held out her hand to stop other chatter as she used the no-debate voice of Walker when he was laying down the law. "'He has to have the ability to keep his rider on, even when they are doing all they can to fall off.'" The ladies laughed hysterically.

"He's not wrong," said Josie. "I can't tell you how many times I have tried to ride a different horse than Crescent with disastrous results."

"Well, you had better breed Crescent and keep his line going. It might be genetic," said Camille.

Their laughter brought the men carrying children back to eat their lunch. The first children to ride and enjoy the three ranches' little menagerie of farm animals would arrive with their escorts at two. They were all ready, but wanted to check again. It was already noon.

Walker pulled Josie in close to wait while the others filled their children's plates first. "We have a good life, don't we, Walker?" asked Josie.

"The best life. I have you all to myself for at least a little while longer. We have plans, and they are good ones. I can't wait for what's in store for us after we get the licenses and certifications needed to do everything. It will be hectic."

Josie nodded. "I know, but it will be gratifying and fulfilling because we will be making a difference."

"Together. We will all be making a difference together."

"Creating a refuge for children in the place that you created one for me. Nothing could be more perfect."

"You couldn't be more perfect. I love you, Josie Knight."

"I love you more, Walker Knight. So much more."

The End

Alyssa Bailey

A lyssa Bailey is a USA Today Bestselling Author of realistic, sensual romance with a touch of suspense. A dyed-in-the-wool Texan living in the splendor of Alaska most of her life, Alyssa now divides her time between the beauty of SE Alaska and the Piney Woods of East Texas. She enjoys taking from her own experiences to create series in realistic locations to tease the reader's palate and invite them to sink into exciting adventures.

Alyssa enjoys writing consensual power exchanges between intelligent, sassy women who are not afraid to make a stand and loving men confident enough to give their woman space but masterful enough to keep her safe and content. There is *always* a "happily ever after."

Visit me online and sign up for my newsletter:
http://alyssabailey.com[1]
Join my Facebook Group for fun and prizes:
https://www.facebook.com/groups/635273300210359/
Find me on Social Media:
https://linktr.ee/alyssabailey

---

1. http://alyssabailey.com/

OTHER BOOKS FROM ALYSSA BAILEY

Safe and Secure Series: Contemporary, suspense, spicy
Saving Sharlee
Saving Jessie
Saving Ivy
Saving Mallory
Saving Callie
Saving Oakley (Sept 2023)
Saving Finley (2023)

Clearwater Daddies -Contemporary, Spicy
Piper's Plan
Camille's Second Chance
Josie's Refuge

Guardians of Refuge (Contemporary Military Spicy)
SEAL of Refuge
The Strategy of Love
The Tactics of Love
The Mandate of Love

Sage County (Contemporary Cowboy Spicy)
Deep Waters
Still Waters

Red Eagle Ranch (Contemporary, multicultural/interracial Spicy)
Stryker's Girl
Declan's Girl
Seamus' Girl
Callen's Girl (TBA)
Carter's Girl (Finally) (TBA)

Anthologies (varies)
Sweet Town Love
Historical Heroes
Multi-Author Box Sets (Heat Level Various)
FREE Book Bites 11
Irresistible Heroes
Tempting Protectors
Love, Christmas 2 Recipes
Unforgettable Protectors (Sept 2023)

Don't miss out!

Visit the website below and you can sign up to receive emails whenever Alyssa Bailey publishes a new book. There's no charge and no obligation.

https://books2read.com/r/B-A-MXIL-WLLIB

BOOKS 2 READ

Connecting independent readers to independent writers.

Did you love *Josie's Refuge (Second chance, Daddy)*? Then you should read *Piper's Plan* by Alyssa Bailey!

Piper has plans, but they defy Daddy's rules. Things could get hot.

Piper Gentry was not one to back down from a challenge, not in her international investments company or in her personal life. Piper looks for sense in her father's death while looking for ways to make the family ranch profitable again in the wild heat of a Texas summer.

Jackson Knight has always loved Piper Gentry. Being her husband and Daddy, raising their family on the ranch is all he has ever wanted, but she never returned from college. Now she's back and his challenge is to remind her that his plans are still her plans and that she feels the same about him. He'll stop at nothing to keep her near him and safe.

Piper's plans do not involve taking orders from anyone, including Jackson, but her longing for what they once had, has her doubting herself. Who will pose the greatest threat to her safety—outsiders eager to get their hands on her family legacy, or Piper herself?

Read more at alyssabailey.com.

Also by Alyssa Bailey

Clearwater Daddies
Josie's Refuge (Second chance, Daddy)

Watch for more at alyssabailey.com.

www.ingramcontent.com/pod-product-compliance
Lightning Source LLC
Chambersburg PA
CBHW060627260626
47161CB00008B/2826